W9-AXV-692

DTS-9.0
RL 5.0

don't expect magic

don't
expect
magic

Kathy McCullough

delacorte press

Text copyright © 2011 by Kathy McCullough
Jacket photograph of girl © 2011 Marianna Massey/Corbis
Jacket photograph of beach scene and photocollage © 2011
Brian Sheridan/Hothouse

All rights reserved. Published in the United States by Delacorte Press, an imprint of Random House Children's Books, a division of Random House, Inc., New York.

Delacorte Press is a registered trademark and the colophon is a trademark of Random House, Inc.

Visit us on the Web! randomhouse.com/teens

Educators and librarians, for a variety of teaching tools, visit us at www.randomhouse.com/teachers

Library of Congress Cataloging-in-Publication Data
McCullough, Kathy.
Don't expect magic / Kathy McCullough. — 1st ed.
p. cm.
Summary: Upon her mother's death, fifteen-year-old Delaney Collins must move to California to live with a father she barely knows, and discovers not only that he is a fairy "godmother," but that she may be one, as well.
ISBN 978-0-385-74012-8 (hc) — ISBN 978-0-385-90824-5 (lib. bdg.) — ISBN 978-0-375-89891-4 (ebook) [1. Fathers and daughters—Fiction. 2. Fairy godmothers—Fiction. 3. High schools—Fiction. 4. Schools—Fiction. 5. Moving, Household—Fiction. 6. Family life—California—Fiction. 7. California—Fiction.] I. Title. II. Title: Do not expect magic.
PZ7.M478414957Don 2011
[Fic]—dc22
2010052996

The text of this book is set in 12-point Apollo MT.

Book design by Angela Carlino

Printed in the United States of America
10 9 8 7 6 5 4 3 2 1
First Edition

Random House Children's Books supports the First Amendment and celebrates the right to read.

for my parents

ACKNOWLEDGMENTS

I'd like to thank the following people, who have performed magic far beyond my expectations: my editor, Wendy Loggia, for helping me make this book into a real novel, and for helping make *me* into a real novelist; Krista Vitola, for cheerfully answering questions both big and small; and Deb Dwyer, for her amazing copyediting. I also want to acknowledge and applaud the expertise of the other Delacorte Press staff members who worked on this book. In addition, I'd like to thank my agents, Lydia Wills and Alyssa Reuben, for their belief in the book and their ongoing encouragement; Julie Schoerke and Marissa DeCuir, for their enthusiasm; my early readers: Mary, Suzy and especially Paula (who endured more bad rough drafts than any devoted cousin should be required to, even if it's her fault I'm a writer); Mark, for his artistry with both words and pictures, and for his business (of life) wisdom; Judy and Dave, for their "animated" brilliance; Mindy and Rebecca, for their friendship and virtuoso detail work; Steven, Marty, Justin, Evan and Tricia, for their cheerleading and support; and all my other friends and family members, who have always rooted for me. Thanks also to my teachers throughout my life, especially Mrs. Q and Mrs. O, and Karen D'Arc, who introduced me to the Society of Children's Book Writers and Illustrators, without which I wouldn't have gotten this far. And finally, I'd like to thank my manager, Dana Jackson, who won't ever give up.

chapter one

Of course I'm cursed with the most uncomfortable seat on the plane. The cushion's deflated in this bizarrely lopsided way, like somebody with one butt cheek exponentially bigger than the other sat there before me and crushed it. My overhead light's burned out and the bald guy in front of me dropped his diet Dr Pepper, splashing sticky soda all over my backpack, which I had wedged under the seat.

It shouldn't be called Murphy's Law, it should be called Delaney Collins's Law, because I'm living it. If something can go wrong, it does, and anything bad just gets worse. I don't even want to be on this plane. But I have no choice.

For now, anyway.

I turn up the volume on my iPod and scroll to the heavy metal playlist Mom downloaded for me: all of her favorite songs for scrambling the brain and numbing the mind. We used to blast it whenever we were angry or depressed or frustrated with the world—which was a lot toward the end. But tonight my brain cells are staying stubbornly unscrambled and unnumbed.

I stare out at the pitch-black night, but the grimy little window just reflects my face back at me. The dim cabin lighting casts weird shadows that make me look like a girl out of a manga book: long black pen strokes for hair, eyes circled in dark ink, face flat and expressionless.

Maybe it's a true reflection. Maybe everything that's happened has drained the human part out of me and left just a two-dimensional drawing.

I wish.

I've tried sketching. I've been working on a new design: thigh-highs with spikes on the backs of the heels, chains around the ankles and slashes up and down the sides like they've been hacked at with a switchblade. I call them Shredded Death. The idea's finished in my head but only halfway done on the page, because my mind keeps getting yanked back . . .

"I like your boots."

I turn away from the window. Next to me in the middle seat is a little girl around four years old. She's in a pink fairy princess outfit, complete with plastic tiara and a magic wand made out of a chopstick with a glitter-covered construction-paper star taped to the end of it. Her over-head light hits her like a spotlight so that she practically shimmers. On her other side, her mother snores softly in the shadows.

I could ignore her. That usually works, but kids and old people can be a problem. There's something abnormal about them—they can't take a hint.

What the hell, I think. Maybe having a pointless conversation with a delusional preschooler will provide the distraction I'm desperate for. It's worth a try. I remove one earbud but keep the other one in, so I'm still getting a regular flow of screeching guitar—an emotional IV.

"Huh?" I say. It's important to start aloof, in case I have to cut it off abruptly. I don't want to lead anyone on, make them think I might actually be friendly.

"I like your boots," the girl says again, and points her lame wand toward my feet. I'm wearing a design I created back in less bleak times. I got the originals from the consignment shop I worked at after school. The boots were too big around the calf, so I slit the leather in the back and then attached brass snaps, with matching ones across the front.

I remember, faintly, the rush of joy I felt painting on the blue and yellow swirls. Mom had wanted me to make her a matching pair. But I never got around to it.

"Thanks."

"Do you like my shoes?" The girl swings out her tiny legs, displaying a pair of sparkly pink flip-flops. Hideous.

I shrug.

"They're magic," she says.

"Uh-huh." Time to turn up the frost. This conversation isn't going anywhere good. I grab the earbud from my lap.

"Can you read my book to me?" The girl holds up the picture book resting on her tray table. She does that sad wide-eyed thing little kids do to get their way. It never works with me. "Pleeease?" She thrusts the book in my face. Annoying.

Even more annoying, I hear myself say, "Sure, whatever."

I sigh. Stuck.

I open the book to its first cheery page and predict that this is *not* going to be a story that sweeps me away. Sure enough, it's one of those sappy girl-lost-in-the-woods, helped-by-the-friendly-talking-animals, magic-spells-broken, evil-ogre-defeated stories. With the traditional but irritating and most dishonest final sentence ever created in the history of literature:

"And she lived happily ever after."

I do my best to inject sarcasm and disapproval into my voice as I read these last words, because even if I'm not going to get anything out of the experience, at least I'll have passed on some wisdom to the younger generation. But the girl just smiles the satisfied smile of one who is hearing the same beloved story for the billionth time. Clearly, I'm going to have to spell it out for her.

"It doesn't really work like that, you know," I tell her. "Things don't end happily."

"Yes, they do."

I shrug and hand the book back to her. "You'll learn," I say. I tried. Someday she'll look back on this conversation and remember she was warned.

"It wouldn't be in the book if it wasn't true," she says firmly, like she's teaching *me* some lesson.

I don't answer. Some people would rather live in a fairy tale.

★ ★ ★

An hour later, I'm standing in the dreary fluorescent-lit baggage claim area as the rest of the passengers from Flight 403 from Newark shove each other and try to figure out which black suitcase is theirs. Mine stands out because I painted red skulls on all four sides. People back away in horror when they see it, conveniently clearing a path for me. As a special bonus, the other passengers keep their distance once I park the suitcase next to my gym bag and sticky backpack. Julie, the flight attendant "in charge" of me, frowns from the opposite side of the carousel, arms crossed, miffed that I refused to bond with her on the plane over her love of hair clips and nail decals. She sees the skulls and shakes her head in further dismay at my failure to fit her sweet teen ideal.

Across the room, near a bolted row of hard plastic chairs, my pink princess seatmate is sitting on a flowery suitcase and reading her book with her mother. Suddenly the girl throws her arms up and squeals, "Daddy!" A man in a long tan coat strides toward her, scoops her up and twirls her around as she shrieks with glee. He's a father from a TV commercial: tall, loving and perfect. He leans over to kiss the mother, and then they all hug. Nauseating.

They pass me on their way to the exit and the little girl waves her wand at me. "I'm giving you a happily-ever-after," she says.

"Thanks, but it'll take more than a chopstick to fix *my* life."

She smiles and moves on, waving the wand at everyone in sight, spreading her imaginary pixie dust all around. I'm relieved when the automatic doors slide shut behind her and her sickening fairy-tale family.

Then I see him. He's at the next carousel. Wearing khakis, a sport coat and a tie, looking stiff and official. I almost expect him to hold up one of those cardboard signs with my name handwritten on it in big block letters. He's shorter than I remember, or I guess I'm taller. He's got a worried expression on his face, and I feel a twinge of something, because the last time I saw him in person I actually *wanted* to. But that's not how I feel now. It's just an automatic reaction, and I immediately will myself to emotionally flatline.

I watch as he gazes around the baggage area, searching. A few people turn and whisper to each other when they see him. One man goes over to him and shakes his hand, and a woman asks him to sign her boarding pass. Unbelievable.

Julie appears at his side and pulls him protectively

away from the mini-crowd. She waves vaguely in my direction and then she launches into her own tale of how he saved her life. I can't hear her, but I recognize the adoring, awed look on her face. As she talks, his glance passes over me, once, twice. I glare at him to help out. His eyes catch mine for a second and quickly shift away—then he slowly turns back. I fold my arms, and finally, he gets it.

After he extricates himself from Julie, he heads my way. He plasters a big smile on his face, exactly like the one that grins out from all of his book jackets. "Delaney . . . ?" he says, his smile twitching a little. It makes me want to scream, *"Who else could I be?!"* but the flight was long and it's late, and I'm too drained right now to summon up the energy.

So I just say, "Hello, Hank." His smile flickers again, then dims, but I don't know why—I haven't called him Dad since I was eleven, and if he thinks I'm going to start now, he's as certifiable as the people who buy his books.

"I almost didn't recognize you," he says, in that fake upbeat tone people use when they're being careful not to insult you directly so you can't call them on it.

"A lot has changed since you last saw me," I reply. "About *four years ago.*"

"I'm really sorry about your mom, Delaney." If I didn't know the pretend-caring thing was part of the whole "Dr. Hank" act, I'd almost believe he was really sad for me. "If I'd had any idea what was going on, I would've come out to help. Why didn't she tell me?"

I shrug. Mom had gotten sick so fast, she didn't have time to make *any* plans. It was like one day she was still the nurse, and then it was *her* in the bed, trapped in the same hospital where she got the infection in the first place. It was up to me to take care of things, and I did it all. Except call Hank.

I told Mom that I'd left messages and that I was sure he'd be on his way soon. But it was a lie. I didn't want him there. Who needed him pacing back and forth and pounding his fist and telling Mom to "think positive" and "be the driver, not the passenger"? I figured he didn't really need to know anyway, because Mom was going to get better, and then it wouldn't matter whether I'd called him or not.

He looks at me as if I'm about to burst into tears or something, and he starts to raise his arms, like we're going to hug. I stare at him with my hostile manga face and he gives up that idea pretty quick. He pats my shoulders instead, but I slither away and drop the strap of my gym bag into one of his outstretched hands. Then I sling on my backpack and wheel my suitcase off toward the exit.

"Uh, I'm actually parked the other way," he says.

I don't answer. I just spin around and march off in the opposite direction. He doesn't say anything else, so I assume I'm going the right way now and that he's following behind me, where he belongs.

chapter two

You might've seen my dad on TV if your parents insist on watching those morning talk shows. He calls himself a life coach, which means people pay him to boss them around. He's also written about a million books with idiotic names like *Fate Is for Fakers* and *Luck Is for Losers* and *How to Stop Whining and Start Living.*

He's on all the covers, usually standing with his foot up on a chair, elbow on his knee, chin resting on his fist. I guess this is his idea of a "can-do" pose or something. Whenever I see it, I want to walk into the photo and kick the chair out from under him.

Mom used to say it wasn't healthy for me to be so

hostile, even if he deserved it, but I think hostility can be good for you. It's like a shot of caffeine. It keeps you sharp. I'm going to need that edge to survive in Sunny Vale, or Happy Valley, or Vomit Del Mar, or whatever the name is of this brainwashed, brain-dead, Stepford Wives town.

Once we get off the freeway, the streets blur past Hank's car window in a video loop of flat square houses with flat square yards, lit by identical streetlights. SUVs sit in every driveway; only their colors are different: black, gray, white, repeat. It's like a toy town. Or a model for a zombie film.

I lean my head out the window. There's even a sweet, perfumey, too-perfect-to-be-real smell to the air. "Night-blooming jasmine," Hank says in a bragging voice, like he personally planted it all.

"I think I might be allergic," I say. I hit the button on the door and the window hums closed. This is a mistake, because now the awkward silence is trapped inside with us and it sucks out all of the oxygen until I feel like I'm suffocating.

"Are you hungry?" Hank asks, his words strained, like he's finding it hard to breathe too. "Would you like to stop for pizza or something?"

"I just want to go to bed." Actually, I'm starving, even though I ate a whole can of potato chips on the plane, along with a cheese-and-cracker plate and a giant walnut cookie. But I'm not in the mood to relive the pizza dinners of the past, where I'd sit across from Hank for the two hours he'd managed to excavate from his book tour appointments and be forced to listen to his coma-inducing speeches about believing in my potential and striving to be self-reliant. As our time ran out, he'd watch me finish off my vanilla ice cream with this queasy, sad look on his face, like I was a puppy he thought was really cute but was allergic to—and like although he felt sorry about having to give me away, he'd rather abandon me than get allergy shots.

But now—ha!—he *has* to take the puppy, and too bad about those allergies.

"Okay," he says brightly. "Home it is!" Home. That's a joke.

A few minutes later, we pull into the driveway of one of the zombie houses. I guess he's able to tell it apart from the others because the outside plants are especially pitiful. A couple of spindly bushes bracket the door like two tumble-weeds, and a few leafless vines cling to the brick above the front window. A moon-sized overhead bulb casts a harsh light on the concrete stoop.

Inside is just as ugh. Lots of beige and brown, and no style. It's all catalog clean and slick and expensive-looking, but it's too dust-free, untouched, unlived-in. I can feel my artistic spirit being sucked right out of me. I cannot, will not, stay here.

It gets worse. Hank leads me down a dim hall to a back bedroom and sets down my suitcase. When he flicks on the light and I see what's inside, I nearly scream. Everything is pink or purple, and there's lace all over the place. Dolls gape at me from the bed. Music boxes and Disney figurines cram the shelves. There's even a canopy bed. Horrifying.

"It's like Cinderella exploded," I say.

Hank gives me a little smile, like we're sharing a joke. "Yeah. I don't know what I was thinking."

"That I was still six years old? I'm *fifteen*."

"I know—"

"And you've *seen* me since I was six. But I guess you never saw my room, did you? Because you never came inside. You were one of those drive-by dads."

Hank cocks his head and studies me. Uh-oh, he's going into Dr. Hank mode. He squints, like he's peering deep into my troubled soul. His lips press together as they await the most piercing, insightful group of sentences *ever* to formulate and then be released to do their magic.

He sits down on the frilly princess bed and pats the spot next to him. I toss my soda-stained backpack at the spot, and he yanks his hand away before it crushes his fingers. He sets the backpack on the floor and then frowns down at his now-sticky hand.

"Delaney, I know you've had a tough few months—"

"Four months, two weeks, three days"—I glance at the enchanted-frog-prince alarm clock—"and sixteen minutes."

Hank takes in a breath and nods, pretending he feels my pain, which is so not remotely possible. "I'm sorry I wasn't there for you. But you're responsible for that, you know. Telling Posh's parents that I said I didn't want you, even though I had no idea what was going on. I really didn't enjoy having Posh's mother spend an hour on the phone yelling at me, by the way."

"So sorry." I still don't understand why Posh's mom couldn't have just believed me, instead of calling Hank behind my back.

"And then refusing to wait for me to fly out and get you." Like I'd want to spend five hours on an airplane stuck next to him.

"I agreed to come, didn't I?"

"You had no choice, Delaney. You're my daughter. You're my legal responsibility." More likely he was worried about what would happen when word got out that the great Dr. Hank had abandoned his motherless offspring. Tabloid headlines. Thousands of copies of his books, shredded. Can't have that happen. Better to take in the semi-orphan, even if you dread it.

"Whatever."

Hank bites his lip and I can tell he's getting pissed off. He clenches his hands a little, like he's trying to keep the rage from leaking out. "It makes sense that you want to take your anger out on me, because I'm the closest target—"

"I'm not taking anything out on you," I tell him calmly. "I feel the same way about you now that I've felt about you for a *loooong* time."

This throws him for a second. He seems to be mentally flipping through his catalog of appropriate Dr. Hank–isms, when his cell phone rings. He scowls down at the number but answers anyway. "Andrea, this is not a good— No, Andrea, listen to me. It's time that you— Yes, I know. . . . No. . . . *Andrea* . . . I'm going to have to call you back."

He hangs up. "Client," he says to me, like I care. I fold my arms, waiting. "Well . . . it's getting late." He claps his hands on his thighs and stands up. "Luckily, we have plenty of time ahead of us to talk about everything."

No, we don't, I think, but I don't say it. Posh's mom wanted me to "give Hank a chance," so part of that act is not letting on that every minute is a countdown till enough time has passed to make it look like I tried.

We stand like that for a second, me at the door and him at the bed, in the opposite places from where we're each supposed to be. He takes a halting step, like he's afraid I might charge him. I don't, though, and I don't block him. Instead I move aside and notice his little twinge of relief as I glide past him to the bed.

"If you need anything, let me know." He waits at the door, one hand on the frame, keeping him in place despite the hostile air pushing him out.

"Nope. I'm good."

Hank winces as I sit and swing my boots onto the brand-new pastel pink bedspread, then lift my sticky backpack up beside me. I plug in my black panther-shaped docking station and crank up the iPod. I wait for Hank to tell me to turn it down. I need my music or I could truly have a mental breakdown, and that's what I'll say if he gives me any flak.

But when I glance over to the door, Hank's already gone, and the door is closed. No goodnight or anything. He's just gone. Blown me off as usual. Not that I expected anything else.

Wait till I tell Posh. I find my phone and send her a text. It's one in the morning back in New Jersey, but she'll still be awake, scouring the net for reports on new quasars or reading a book on rare marsupials and using her lime-green highlighter to mark the passages she wants to read later.

Posh Slikowski and I are best friends by default. We met in detention. Posh has "behavioral issues," while I'm just a smart-ass, according to most of my teachers. Posh was in a special ed class for a while, which was pretty perverted considering she has the highest GPA in the school. Her parents sued the district and now she has an aide who follows her around from class to class and tries to get her to stop talking, but good luck.

While I wait for her to call, I go back to working on my new boot design. I tap my pencil against the page, hoping for inspiration. I'm not going to find it in this room, though, unless I want to make a pair of pink sequined boots with blond princesses etched into the sides. My sparkly wand-wielding seatmate from the plane might like them, and she'd love this room, but I feel like I've been trapped in Oz.

I could've let Posh's parents ship out some of my stuff, but I'm not staying, so I'd only have to ship it back again. It's all in a storage locker somewhere with Mom's things and the furniture from our apartment and . . . I don't like thinking about it.

I turn up the volume on the iPod so the bed is practically vibrating. A few seconds later, there's a knock. Ha. I knew it. I knew he'd be back to lecture me.

"Delaney?"

I turn down the music, a little. "Yessss?" I say sweetly.

"I have to run out for a bit."

This isn't what I'm expecting. I'm tensed up for a fight and now that energy's got nowhere to go. I turn the volume lower.

"Where?"

"I have to help a client with something." He sounds unsure, or maybe it's just that his voice is muffled by the door.

"Really," I say. "Right now."

"It's kind of urgent. I have my phone if you need me. You don't have to wait up."

"Why would I wait up?" I say. Nothing from the other side of the door. After a beat, his footsteps fade down the hall.

I move to the window and peer out through the curtains to the driveway. There's a muffled click as the front door closes, and then I see Hank cross to the car. I don't get it. What kind of life coach makes house calls at ten-thirty on a Wednesday night? And on the same night his only daughter has come to visit him for the first time in forever?

As Hank's car pulls out, the headlights flash over my face and I drop the curtain.

Weird.

★ ★ ★

It's midnight and Hank's still not back. Posh never called. She must've left her phone in the library again.

I try to sleep, but it's impossible to even relax in this room. The sheets are too stiff, the pillow's too soft, and I feel like I'm being suffocated by cuteness. I should be crashing because of the time change, but nights are the worst. My brain just spins and spins. No way I can sketch or read when it gets like this, so I don't even try. I could watch a video on my iPod, but instead I flip open my phone and call up the photos.

I scroll through them. Mom with chocolate all over her face at Hershey Park. Mom yelling when I got suspended for stealing library books, eyes bugging out, her mouth scary wide. She hated that picture at first, but later she thought it was hilarious. Mom and I cheek to cheek after getting bad haircuts at the mall. Mom smiling at me from her hospital bed. I don't notice the tears until I see them land on the screen. I thumb them off and then swipe my palm over my face.

I'm pressing the stop key to turn off the phone, when it rings. "POSH," the screen reads, over a photo I took of her last Halloween when she dressed up as Valentina Tereshkova, the Russian cosmonaut. I answer. "Final—"

As usual, I can't even get a whole word in. "Oh my God, Delaney. I'm so sorry. I didn't notice your message. I've been glued to the NASA live feed. You would not believe the nanoflares around these coronal loops they're showing. Check out NASA-dot-gov-slash-topics-slash-solar-system-slash—"

"I'm not at my computer, Posh."

"Oh, right. Okay. I'll send you the link. Hold on."

Posh keeps gushing about nebulae and light-refracting subatomic something, still in outer space. Hearing Posh's voice makes me miss her so bad. She's the only person I can talk to and she's clear across the country. I can't count down any longer. I need to get home. Right now.

". . . so that's three-fifty-seven your time. Look in the lower southwest quadrant of the sky."

"Posh," I practically shout, trying to get her back to earth. "I have to get out of here. You've got to talk to your parents." I open my door. Hank's left all the lights on and it takes a second for my eyes to adjust. I step out and head down the hall, bringing the phone with me. "Tell them they have to let me come back."

"But you just got there."

In the living room, I check anything with drawers or a lid. Decorative boxes. End tables. I find coasters with beach scenes on them, more letter openers than anyone needs and a set of old-fashioned fountain pens, but no cash.

"One day's all I needed. Not even a day." Across the hall from the living room is the dining room. There's a cabinet against one wall, but there's no secret compartment behind the wineglasses or lockbox in the drawers under the leaf-print napkins. "He's already abandoned me again."

"What? You're kidding!" I've finally gotten her attention.

"I know, right?" The kitchen's another lifeless showroom, with marble counters and cooking-show-worthy appliances. Lots of cupboards and drawers, the utensils and silverware neatly lined up inside organizer-store dividers.

"As soon as we got here, he's like, 'I have to go see a client.'" One drawer is all take-out menus and loads of chopsticks. I throw everything out on the counter. "In the middle of the night? What's *that* about?"

I remember hearing that some people keep their money in the fridge. I open both doors and dig around, but all I find is about a thousand stacked boxes of "lite" frozen entrées, six-packs of souped-up yogurt and a bunch of premade salads and bean-sprouty-looking sandwiches. There's no plastic cabbage with a hidden compartment and no roll of twenties in the butter dish. There's also nothing remotely appetizing. I slam the doors.

"Oh my God," Posh says. "It's probably not a client. It's probably a *girlfriend*."

"Ugh." I shudder at the thought.

On the other side of the living room is the den, but there's nothing in it except a tan vinyl couch, a silver floor lamp, a flat-screen TV and a glass coffee table with a remote perfectly centered on top of it. "I can't imagine what kind of brainless hag would go out with him." I snatch up the remote and toss it onto the couch just because.

"Uh, well, Delaney, you know . . . your mom . . ."

Right. *Mom*. She went out with Hank, obviously. But he must've been less of a loser then, right? I say this to Posh.

"Sure!" she chirps, relieved I'm not upset. Posh doesn't do emotion very well.

Heading back down the hall, I spot a closed door across from my room. "Well, he doesn't have to worry about me getting in the way of his skanking around. I'm gone as soon as I can dig up some cash." The door's unlocked. I turn the light on and smile.

Jackpot. Hank's home office.

Copies of Hank's books line one wall of shelves, and multiple miniatures of Hank's face beam out at me from the spines. The desk is shiny clean, like it's ready to pose for one of Hank's book covers. The only thing not work-related in the room is a framed photo, but it's of a carnival pier at sunset. There aren't even any people in it. I'd expect him to at least have some fake friends—one or two celebrity-obsessed suck-ups. It's all kind of sad. Or it would be if I cared.

"The plane fare's like hundreds of dollars," Posh tells me. "Plus, you can't just walk into an airport and buy a ticket. They'd see your ID and know you're not eighteen."

"Then I'll take a bus." I open the top drawer of the desk and dig around. Nothing but phone bills, receipts and scribbled notes. The next drawer is office supplies. "Or I could hitchhike."

"You can't do that!" The panicked whine Posh gets when she's starting to flip out builds in volume. "You'll never make it alive! It's nothing but freaks and perverts out there. You'll end up chopped in little pieces, stuffed in a bus locker or buried out in the middle of the desert!"

"Okay, okay, Posh. Calm down." The bottom drawer is the largest. I tug on the handle, but it won't open. There's no lock, it's just overstuffed. Maybe this is his emergency earthquake fund. I picture banded stacks of fresh bills, like a movie criminal's stash.

I set the phone down on the carpet. Posh's voice is now a tiny buzz as she begs me to wait and tells me that she's worried about me taking the bus alone because buses have freaks and perverts too. I wedge my feet against the legs of the desk and grab the handle of the drawer with both hands. I'm about to yank when I hear a noise down the hall.

It's the front door. I jump up and snap off the light. Posh's words continue to spill out of the phone in a rush: she swears she's going to work on her parents until they give in. She promises, promises, promises, and I have to believe her, pleeeease.

I snatch up the phone. "I do," I whisper, "I know you will. I have to go. Hank is home."

All my moves are careful and quiet: putting down the phone, dashing across the hall to my room, holding the knob on the door as I close it and then slowly releasing it so the bolt slides in without a sound.

I wait. Hank's footsteps approach, then pause. I hear the office door click shut. Hank takes another step and I sense him standing outside my door, listening, debating whether to knock. My heartbeat counts the seconds, crashing louder and louder in my ears, until, finally, the footsteps resume and fade, and I can breathe again.

Back in bed, I keep my eyes wide open. I'll wait about a half hour and then peer out into the hall. If it's safe, if all the lights are out, I'll sneak back into the office and check out that last drawer. I know I'm going to find what I need in there.

My eyes blink, trying to close. I take deep breaths to wake myself up, but my energy seeps out of me, into the bed, pulling me with it . . . down, down. Words and thoughts flutter through my mind, but they don't stick. They just dissolve, like moth wings, and I can't fight it anymore.

I'm out.

chapter three

In the morning, I wake up so tired I'm drenched with it, and at first I can't remember anything. Where I am or even who I am.

I stare up at the bizarre canopy over my head, and images from my dreams come back. Flowering vines growing wildly and strangling me. Princess dolls that have come to life, forming an army of pink-clad zombies. Hank being left on a front stoop, abandoned and forlorn, as I drive off with Mom, who has come to my rescue.

I blink and blink, expecting to wake up back in my room, with Mom calling out that I'm late for breakfast, but it's a man's voice I hear, and I realize that I *am* awake.

Then it all comes back, like it always does, memory after memory, fast-forwarding to the present, even when I try to stop it before it gets to the stuff I want to forget.

Taking a shower washes away some of the fog. The bathroom off my room is all white and more white. Towels, soap, toothbrush holder. Even the wicker wastepaper basket's been spray-painted white. It's soulless, but at least it's not pink. By the time I'm dressed, I feel almost semiconscious, which is pretty good for me.

When I open my door, I can hear Hank in the kitchen, humming along to some oldies rock-and-roll station. I consider a quick slip into his office, but Hank leans his head into the hall and sees me.

"Good morning!" His voice booms down at me, so fast and loud I feel like I should duck. I hope he doesn't expect conversation—I don't do mornings. "Did you sleep well?" I grunt in response. He waves a big, cheery "Come on" wave. I grab my backpack and trudge toward him.

On the kitchen table, Hank has lined up five brand-new boxes of cereal, the types that are all sugar and shaped like stars or little bears and have cheap plastic toy pirates inside. Further proof that he still has me trapped in his memory as a kindergartner. What's next? A bag lunch? A Little Mermaid lunch box packed with string cheese and apple slices?

The bears are actually my favorite, though, so I pour myself a bowl. I make sure to roll my eyes at Hank so he won't know I like them.

"I called the school yesterday," he tells me. "They have your records. You just have to pick up your schedule from the office." He waits for a thank-you at this fatherly bit of taking charge, but I don't respond because I know it was Posh's mom who had the records sent.

He sits down across from me. "Were you looking for anything in particular last night?" I pause midchew as I get a flashback of the mess I made in the kitchen and living room during my money quest. I flick a glance at the counters, but everything's been put away. He must've gotten up before dawn to clean—nothing can be out of place in Dr. Hank's world. It must be driving him crazy that I don't fit anywhere. That he can't stick me in some closet cubbyhole and close the door.

"No." This seems like the safest answer.

Hank nods knowingly, even though I know he doesn't know. He clasps his hands together, resting them on the table. "If you need something, Delaney, you just have to ask me."

"Okeydokey." I smile without meaning it and slurp my green-tinted milk.

Hank frowns a moment, but then quickly puts his "I'm very interested" expression back on. "So. *Is* there anything you'd like to discuss?"

He's not going to leave it alone. Okay, I'll play. "Yeah," I say. "How was your *client*?"

Hank leans back and drops the intense gaze. "Fine." He pushes away from the table and looks anywhere except at me as he carries the cereal boxes back to the cupboard. "I'm sorry I had to go out, but it's part of my job. The kind of coaching I do, I have to be on call around the clock."

"Uh-huh." It's got to be a girlfriend, but why not tell me? How long does he think he can hide it? Maybe he's just waiting, like I am, for me to leave.

I stand, finished with breakfast and the conversation. Hank tells me that the school is a few streets down and offers to give me a ride.

"I'll skate," I say. Before he can ask how, I answer by snapping down the retractable wheels on my snake boots.

Hank's eyebrows go up in surprise and he leans to the side to get a better look. "I've seen the sneakers with wheels, but I didn't know there were boots too."

"I made them."

"Really?" He's circling me now, and I can tell he's impressed. I almost smile but I catch myself in time. I don't want him to think his opinion matters.

There's another weird silence, like at the bedroom door last night. It's kind of hilarious: Dr. Hank, the man who always knows what to say, saying nothing. It would be funnier if I were watching it instead of living it, if I didn't keep feeling so trapped.

Once again, it's up to me to make the first move, so I spin around and shove my chair under the table. "Is school right or left?" I ask, pointing an index finger in either direction.

Hank perks up, in charge once more. "It's five blocks west."

"I'm not a compass," I say, and wave my fingers so he'll pick one. He points to my right.

"You pass Poinsettia and then Orchid. There's a light at Rosewood and then two more blocks . . ." He falters as I glide by him to the dining room, backpack on my shoulder, on my way. "It'll be on the corner—" My skates clack and whir on the wood floors, through the front hall to the door, drowning out his final words. "—on your left!"

Outside, it's pure solar torture. I can't see the sun, but it's definitely up there, dialed to maximum wattage, turning the sky an insane crystal blue. You need industrial sunglasses and I don't even have ordinary ones. It's not helping my jet lag, my Category 5 headache or my mood.

I slowly start to feel more awake as I soar down the street. The air is cool and smells honey-sweet, and there's a fruity scent too, like a tangerine that's just been peeled. It cuts through my brain haze and clears my head.

In the daylight, I notice there are slight differences in the houses. Bay windows that are curved on top and others that are square. Front stoops or flat walks. A bunch of the houses have big bushy vines draped over one wall, with flowering bursts at the ends—fuchsia on one house, blood-red on the next, and then orange, lavender, pale pink—colors so bright they look painted on. It's pretty, I guess, but it's still too perfect, like a doll town for giants.

Clusters of kids appear, in cars or on foot, heading to

the end of the block. The noise builds, chatter and laughter and yelled greetings, and I feel stupidly excited. Maybe I'm light-headed from too little sleep, but I'm actually looking forward to school. It's the one thing that's familiar.

I sail around the corner—and then skid to a stop.

Up ahead, beyond a dazzling green treated-with-carcinogenic-chemicals front lawn, stands the high school, all pinky-red brick and sandblasted white stone. Palm trees loom and sway like mop-topped giraffes. It's another movie set, this one from one of those idiotic TV "family" films. The kids are even dressed in pastel colors, like walking Easter M&M's.

The green snakes on my boots are the only color in my outfit, other than the silver on my chain belt and on my dog-collar bracelet. To say I stand out from the crowd is the understatement of the millennium. There's not a speck of black anywhere.

Two quasi-Goths slump against the wall near the entrance, but even they're dressed in violet, with matching lilac eye shadow and lipstick. They glance over at me, wary and semi-alarmed. I guess I do look like I just beamed down from Pluto. They don't realize that *they're* the ones who are the pod people.

My earlier idiotic eagerness is officially dead. I can already tell that inside it's going to be all gung-ho teachers and pep rallies and National Honor displays and seasonal hall decorations. Ugh. I should just head back to Hank's and hide outside until it's safe for me to sneak into his office and grab the money I know is in that desk drawer. If he doesn't go out, I'll wait until he's in the kitchen making lunch or something and then climb in through the window. I don't have to go back to my bedroom. Everything I need is in my backpack: my sketchbook and my music. It's better to travel light. And if I have money, I can buy stuff along the way. I'll take the train instead of a bus. I'm a pro at that. Mom and I used to take the train all the time. What am I waiting for? Would anyone even know if I never showed up to class? Or care?

CLICK CLICK CLICK.

I turn around to see a guy my age a few yards away, in an oversized army jacket, pointing a camera the size of a truck at me. He's got a dozen more cameras slung around his neck as he click-click-clicks away.

I shoot daggers into the lens and he finally lowers the behemoth. "Hey!" he shouts, like he's just noticed me. "You're new, right? Mind if I take a couple of pictures for yearbook?" He raises the camera again and adjusts the focus.

I skate up to him and put my palm over the lens. He pulls the camera away and frowns. "Uh, you shouldn't actually touch the glass," he says. "The surface is very sensitive."

He takes a small square leather case out of his jacket pocket, opens it and lifts out a tiny squirt bottle and an even tinier gauzy white cloth. He carefully cleans the lens like he's performing brain surgery on a mouse. Definitely a dork.

I feel something bearing down from above. I gaze up and then shield my eyes. The sun has risen enough to see now, like it had to prove its existence. Or maybe it just wants to torment me, like everybody else.

"What's with the sky here?" I ask Camera Boy. It's actually bluer than it was earlier—I didn't even think that was possible. It's the definition of deep blue, and I don't mean dark blue. I mean like you could drown in it if you let it suck you in.

He glances up and smiles. "Oh, it's always like that. Pretty sweet, huh?"

I shudder, horrified. "How can you stand it?" He turns back to me, confused, but I'm done with the chat. I need cover from all this sunshine, from the bright colors and beautiful smells that scream "Be happy!" The closest indoor space is the school, so I decide to stick it out for now. I'll get the money tonight, after Hank goes to sleep, and sneak out at dawn. That's a better plan.

I push off and skate toward the entrance. Behind me I hear Yearbook Guy clickety-clicking, but I'm in motion, so he's going to end up with nothing but blur.

As I feared, the halls are painted a cheerful baby blue and there are exclamation-point-heavy posters everywhere, praising the latest Green Warrior of the Month and cheering the all-state coed tetherball team, and urging everyone to say "No!" to nonrecycled paper and "Yes!" to sunscreen. The kids are way too awake and upbeat for pre–eight a.m. incarceration. I'm used to grumbling and hunching and pale pillow-creased faces. And where's the washed-out green glare of the fluorescent overheads? I glance up to the ceiling. I can't believe it. There are actually skylights. Even inside, the sun shines here. It's not natural.

At least the office is right next to the front door, so I don't have to ask any of the pastel-clad natives for directions. The secretary smiles at me as she hands me my schedule and locker assignment, but her eyes flick from my belt to my boots and I can tell the smile is only barely covering a "what some parents today let their children get away with" frown. Whatever.

"You must be Delaney!" A freakishly tall ponytailed man in black jeans and a Hawaiian shirt bounds out of the back office. He grabs my hand and shakes it. "I'm Principal Rosenthal, but you can call me Lee." He waves to one of the chairs against the wall and then takes the seat next to me, the smell of cigarettes plus spearmint wafting off him.

"So sorry to hear about your loss." His face droops in super-sadness, like he's donned the Mask of Tragedy. A quarter of a second later, Comedy's back, though: huge beaming smile, eyes curved into delighted half-moons. "But we're *so* glad to have you here at Allegro. You're going to love it. And I want you to feel free to come in and see me anytime, Delaney, whether it's to get advice on making friends or help in adjusting to a different way of life. I think you'll find that we're a little more laid-back here." He leans back as if to demonstrate, and then glances at my crossed arms and at the heel of my boot, which I'm tapping on the floor impatiently. "We operate at a slower pace." I unfold my arms, stop the tapping and try leaning back like Laid-Back Lee, but it just makes me more anxious.

I refold my arms and go back to tapping. I want to get to class already, get on with it. Principal Lee continues with the welcome speech anyway. "We have lots of fun electives to choose from," he says, and forces a typed-up list on me. "They're all wonderful opportunities to interact and blend." Blend? What am I, a fruit smoothie? "You can go to the library for seventh period until you pick one." He leaps up from his seat like a giant grasshopper and reaches out for my hand again. "Don't forget: my door is always open. 'Principal' is just a long way of saying 'pal.' So stop by whenever the mood strikes. Will you do that for me, Delaney?"

"Uh, sure."

"Great!" Principal Pal Lee beams, relieved. I'm relieved too, to get out of here. I never thought I'd miss Mrs. Buckston, aka the Hornet, our bitter, teenager-hating principal at East Lombard, my school in New Jersey. She may have operated at nonstop-scream level and handed out unfair punishments like confetti, but at least she never tried to be your "friend."

My first class is AP Chem I: Room 135, Mr. McElroy. I've only got like a minute before it starts, but I lower my wheels and zigzag easily through the stragglers, skidding up to the door just as the bell rings. Perfect timing.

Except some idiot steps in front of me before I've

stopped and—*SMASH!*—we collide. I clutch the door-frame for balance as the moron tumbles backward. Cameras spin around his neck like a pinwheel and crash down on top of him.

It's the blue-sky-loving dork from yearbook.

"Watch where you're going, photo freak," I tell him. He struggles to gather up his cameras before they're crushed underfoot by a couple of tanned lifeguard types, who shoot an amused look down as they enter the room. Their gaze shifts to me, but it doesn't stay long, just long enough for me to catch the "whoa, you don't belong *here*" vibe. Tell me something I don't know.

"I'm not the one breaking the law," Yearbook Guy snaps at me. "No Rollerblades inside the school. It's a safety hazard."

I slam the toes of each boot on the floor so the wheels retract and I'm no longer committing a deadly school-hallway felony. I toss Camera Boy an "are you satisfied?" smirk, but he's gone back to detangling and isn't paying attention anymore.

In the classroom, the disapproving stares from the hallway have multiplied. Everyone's wearing one except the teacher, Mr. McElroy, a short guy with a pudgy face and droopy eyes, who has no expression at all. "I'm a transfer," I tell him, and hand him my admission slip. Out in the hall, Mr. Paparazzo's still having trouble untangling his camera straps. "From a distant, more highly evolved culture."

"We're honored to have you among us, Ms. . . ." Mr. McElroy glances at the slip. ". . . Collins. I'm sure your presence will enlighten and enrich us all." I give him a look. Is he mocking me? It's hard to tell with that face. "You can partner with Flynn Becker. Table six." Mr. McElroy points to a lab table at the back of the room. "Fittingly, we're studying acidic properties today." Okay, that was sarcasm for sure. I meet his eyes, but he keeps a straight face. I like this guy. He's got an edge. He's definitely not from this sugarcoated land of smiles and sunshine.

I mentally brush away the curious stares and whispers as I walk back to my table, which I'm relieved to find is empty, even though it's meant for four people, two on each side. Whatever the other three are out sick with, I hope it's chronic.

Camera Boy finally enters, his camera straps now slung over each shoulder like climbing ropes. He holds up his palm, warding off a scolding from Mr. McElroy, who is frowning at his watch. "I was involved in a major collision," Camera Boy says. "Property damage *and* personal trauma."

Mr. McElroy shakes his head, unimpressed. "Take it up with your insurance agent. I'd like to start class." Camera Boy shrugs and heads to the back. "Oh, by the way, Flynn," Mr. McElroy calls after him, "you have a lab partner now. Delaney Collins."

Camera Boy freezes; then his eyes shift to me, his look filled with dread.

"Great," I say to myself.

"Great," I hear Flynn say under his breath at the same time.

He trudges over next to me and gently sets down his cameras on the ledge under the cabinets that line the wall. This takes about five hours as he carefully lines each one up and makes sure none are touching. I expect him to pet them next, or kiss them on the top of their little black plastic heads. Instead he shoots me a wannabe lethal glare. "The fish-eye lens on my SLX 4700 is cracked."

"Sue me," I say.

"I might." He starts to get worked up. "I have physical evidence *and* witnesses. I could take you to any court and—"

I lean in close to his face. "Here's the deal: you don't talk to me, I don't talk to you. You don't get strangled with one of your camera straps, I don't have to listen to your whining."

Flynn blinks. He opens his mouth, closes it. I've made my point. But then he opens it again. "We *have* to talk," he protests. "We're lab partners. We have to write up our reports together and—"

"I'm not going to be here long. This is just a temporary stopover."

Flynn pulls his notebook out of his backpack. "Too bad you had to set your broom down at all," he mumbles. He might not have wanted me to hear him, but I did.

So I say, in a voice even softer than his but clear enough

35

so he'll get every word, "You better watch out or your fish-eye isn't going to be the only thing that's cracked."

Flynn doesn't say anything or even glance in my direction, but he carefully takes several tiny steps away from me, cramming himself closer to the corner of the table with his cameras.

I get a sour feeling, like I've stomped on a spider that really didn't do anything wrong except be alive where I could see it and smush it without stopping to think first. It's not like me to feel remorse for no reason, and I try to shake the feeling off. Flynn will be fine, I tell myself. I've actually done him a favor, because now he'll stay far, far out of my way, where it's safe.

"Okay, people," Mr. McElroy says. "Chapter Four. Acid-base reactions. Let's get out beakers, pipettes and lab trays. I'll be passing out bottles of HCl." He pushes a rolling cart from table to table and sets a fat glass bottle on the end of each.

Behind him, the classroom door opens, and two girls come in. One is tall, with long shampoo-commercial shiny black hair and an electric-red miniskirt. The other has her artfully highlighted blond hair up in a ponytail and is wearing a yellow bubble dress. I mentally nail their types immediately: self-centered supermodel and her perky sidekick. They chatter and giggle with a few eardrum-piercing squeals thrown in as they stroll past the tables.

"So I told her, I really, really love the hoops on you,"

Supermodel is saying to Perky, "but, like, if you got a bob, then they would just really pop." With her long legs and silky hair, she seems to walk in slow motion. Right and left, all of the boys and a few of the girls look on the verge of fainting from lovelorn lust. Unbelievable.

"Oh my God, that was, like, totally the perfect thing to say because it actually sounds, you know, like a compliment," says Perky.

"I know! And I really meant it!" Mr. McElroy's staring his dry, expressionless stare right at them, but they're in airhead oblivion. "She's going to get it done today at Anton's at the mall and finally the whole squad'll be equally gorgealicious."

"You're so selfless—"

"Excuse me, ladies," Mr. McElroy says. "This is not a chat room, it's a class. And it started ten minutes ago."

"Oh, I'm so sorry, Mr. McElroy!" Supermodel says, and makes it sound "like *totally!*" sincere. "I have a note." She hands Mr. McElroy a slip of paper and she and Perky stride off—to the other side of our table. Table 6 has gone from a temporary oasis to the officially worst place in the room to be. Why is my luck *always* so bad?

Mr. McElroy reads Supermodel's note and for the first time his expression changes, to a sort of mystified disbelief. " 'Emergency Pep Council summit'?" He looks over at Supermodel, who shrugs and smiles sweetly, and Mr. McElroy lets it go, of course. Just once I'd like to see one of those popular-perfect girls get detention.

"Hi, Flynn," Supermodel says, and flashes her movie-star smile at Flynn. There's a bright bounce in her voice as if finding Flynn at this table is just the *most* delightful surprise *ever,* although aren't they across from each other every day?

Flynn gives her a "Hey" and a little wave but concentrates on setting up our lab equipment. He's the one other person in the room besides me who doesn't seem ready to collapse at Supermodel's feet and pledge eternal devotion. I give him a quarter of a point for good judgment and vow not to say anything threatening for the rest of the period as his reward.

"Oh, hi! Are you new?" I glance up to see that Super-model's got her high-beam smile aimed my way now. "I'm Cadie Perez." She leans past Flynn before I even realize what's going on, grabs my hand and gives it an enthusiastic shake, like she really is glad to meet me. "This is Mia." Cadie gestures to Perky, who offers me a frosty wave. I say nothing, as expressionless as Mr. McElroy, but Cadie goes right on. "You should totally feel free to ask us if you have any questions about school, or, like, where to hang out, or whatever." She smiles again, my hostility ricocheting right off her friendly force field. Weird.

Mr. McElroy sets the HCl bottles on our tables. "Are we done with the social networking? Or would you four prefer to stay after school and complete the experiment then?"

"Oh, we can't do that, Mr. McElroy," Cadie says, apparently impervious to sarcasm as well as hostility. "We have an away game at Valley Glen."

"Then let's get to work. *Please.*"

Cadie grins goofily over at me, like we're in cahoots. I roll my eyes and she laughs, unaware that I'm rolling them at *her.*

Cadie and Mia pull out their notebooks and fill the airspace with their mindless chatter about cheerleading and some girl's crush on a drummer in the school band and a new reality show set at a makeup counter that is just *so* educational. Meanwhile, Flynn measures and pours and writes down numbers and equations, completely focused, as if I'm not there at all.

All around me, kids are hunched over, eyes on their beakers or pipettes. This is not the way I wanted to be left alone. This is like I'm invisible. Like I've disappeared but I'm still here, stuck, trapped in this candy-colored, pretty-people parallel universe, surrounded by strangers. The feeling I had last night when I talked to Posh returns. The need to escape, to fly out of here, back to where I belong.

An image comes to me in a flash. I grab my sketchbook and the pencil practically moves on its own as the picture in my mind materializes on the page. Falcon boots. With wings that unfold from the sides and tiny rocket engines in the heels. They're a total fantasy, of course, but I can't help wondering if they could really work.

"Ms. Collins." Mr. McElroy stands at the head of our lab table, arms folded. "In your distant, more highly evolved culture, they may let you do whatever you want in class, but we simple, backward folk expect students to stick to the subject matter being taught." I'm not invisible anymore. Now everybody in class is staring. This makes me want to jet away even faster. "You might even find that doing the work helps you feel better."

An angry heat rises into my cheeks and I snap my sketchbook shut. "I feel fine."

Mr. McElroy's flat expression doesn't change, except that his eyebrows arch a mini-micromillimeter. "Then you'll feel even better than fine, and who wouldn't want that?" His brows poke up a little more, then go back in place, and he moves off to bother the kids at the next table.

Flynn peers at me, sideways. I remember my pledge and swallow the urge to snap, "What are *you* looking at?" Instead I say, "You were right. I guess we *do* have to talk." It's only fifteen minutes to the end of class. I can hold out that long.⌝

Flynn hesitates, regarding me with caution, but when there's no sarcastic follow-up, he pushes a sheet of paper over to me. On it, the steps of the experiment are all laid out. "I'm up to number four."

We get through the assignment with the bare minimum of words exchanged. When the bell rings, I'm the first one out the door. I'm tempted to return to Plan A and abandon ship, but Principal Lee is roaming the halls, bonding and befriending. I'm trapped. No problem, though. I remind myself that I'm the invisible girl. I'll just mentally check out, and before I know it, the day will be over and Happy High will be history.

But my cloak of invisibility doesn't last. In French II, a witch named Madame Kessler has me read aloud from some poem about a giant and then says my accent is *"trop canadien,"* which is *"pas bon du tout,"* sparking veiled smirks from a couple of cashmere-clad French snobs sitting in front of me and snickers from *les autres* losers *dans la classe.*

In world history, I have to sit on the window ledge until an extra chair can be brought in—which happens right when the bell rings. Then the trig teacher, Mr. Nisonson, who must've been the hazing king at his college fraternity, makes me come up to the board and determine the range and domain of an inverse sine function, even after I tell him we were only up to reciprocal functions in my school. "I'll talk you through it," he says, but the way he does it is so confusing that I end up seeming like a math-impaired moron. So now, on top of all the wary and freaked and unfriendly looks I've already been getting, I have to suffer through a bunch of pitying "it's sad she's so stupid but why did they put her in this class?" ones too.

Gym is bizarre. Instead of the usual deadly bullet sports like volleyball and basketball, they teach *yoga* here. Ms. Byrd's got everybody down on blue mats, doing *supta padangusthasana.* Everybody except me, since I don't have the proper "yogi-wear." Ms. Byrd gives me a business card for the Tranquility Den, where the school gets a discount, and then makes me sit in the bleachers and practice my breathing. Right. Like I need to practice when I've been doing it since birth.

I figure that at least lunch will be a break from the torture. A chance for me to find some empty corner where no one will pay any attention to me and I can sketch and listen to music and be alone. Ha. First of all, the lunchroom is *outside*. The "cuisine stations," which is what they call the food lines, are inside, but then you have to carry your food through these tall sliding glass doors to a fancy tiled patio. Around the perimeter, there's a roof frame, with a rolled-up tarp for the one day every other century that it rains. A squadron of heat lamps stand guard against the wall, for those chilly below-eighty-degree days.

You bring your food outside—if you *have* any food, that is. I forgot to bring money, and Hank didn't bother to give me any, of course, so my lunch is a tiny bag of pretzels that I stuffed in my backpack on the plane and forgot about until now. There's nowhere for me to sit and eat them, though. There's no far end of a half-populated bench that I can slide onto and be left alone, because there are no benches, only big backyard-barbecue-type round tables. This wouldn't be so bad if there were at least an Island of Misfits table, but no luck. At East Lombard, there was always a table where the cliqueless sat. The smelly kid, the aggressively ugly girl, the boy who talked to himself, the girl who looked like a walking corpse, and other assorted untouchables. They didn't interact, but they were bonded by their lowest-of-the-low misery.

Here at Happy High, however, there are no true outcasts. There are a few geeks with bulky glasses and skinny ties, some mopey girls with braces and bad hair, and a handful of boys in acne purgatory, but none of them are alone. They sit together with members of their own kind, at their own tables, laughing and chatting and slurping their sodas blissfully.

The cheerleader types take up two tables, pushed together to form a bulky figure eight. Cadie sees me and waves to an empty chair sitting at the crack between the tables. Mia shoots me a "you better not" glare. She doesn't need to worry. Even with no lunch, I'd end up gagging from the bleach-brained conversation and designer shampoo fumes.

Flynn's at one of the neither-outcast-nor-popular tables, with a couple of equally oddball-looking guys, plus a trio of hypersmiley girls with matching Hello Kitty backpacks. He glances toward me, like he's debating saying something. It's not an invitation to join them, because there's no room at their table—not that I'd sit there if there were.

I could find some shady space around the side of the building, but I'd still be outside and the sun would still be shining, and I'm really not in the mood. Instead I slip back inside, past the food lines, through the door to the empty hallway. There's a girls' bathroom at the far end of the school, with a window ledge big enough for me to sit on, and a screen that filters out the sun and makes the sky look gray. It's the one place I've found in the school that has fluorescent lights.

It's dim inside, and echoey and depressing, and there's no room to sketch, but at least I get my wish to be left alone. I can almost imagine, as I eat my tiny stale pretzel twists and gaze out through the dusty screen, that I'm back home in New Jersey. Soon I will be, I tell myself, and the thought cheers me up a little and makes me forget, for a second, where I am.

Unfortunately, it's a smash cut to reality for sixth period: Brit lit, Ms. Sandor. The stares from the other kids are endless; the whispering is nonstop. It's like the whole school has formed a pact against the invader. Cadie's in the class, but even she's turned against me. No attempt to say hello, no smile, nothing. Ms. Sandor has us read a bunch of Elizabeth Barrett Browning poems with titles like "The Cry of the Children" and "A Thought for a Lonely Death-Bed." Just what I need to cheer me up. The fifty minutes drag on like fifty hours before the agony finally ends.

I still have to get through seventh period: electives. I'm on the way to the library when I notice that, for once, the halls are Principal Lee–free. Hmm. There's nowhere I officially have to be. There's no attendance sheet with my name on it. . . .

"Bell's about to ring, you know." I turn around and see Flynn at the far end of the hall, watching me. He's lost the wariness and is back to the curious look he gave me this morning, when I first saw him outside school. I almost say, "Take a picture, it'll last longer," but then I realize he probably would.

"Thanks for the update."

"Seventh period is electives, you know. Did you pick an elective?"

It's probably best not to tell him that I've elected to leave early. "I'm going to the library. I better hurry, because rumor has it the second bell's about to ring."

Flynn grins to let me know he gets the joke, but I didn't say it to amuse him, I said it to get rid of him. "Okay, then. See you tomorrow, partner." He tips an imaginary hat, slips into the classroom behind him and closes the door. Then the second class bell does ring. It's the final bell for me. I'm free. I head down the hall, away from the library, away from Flynn, away from the hell that is Happy High.

I spot a side exit and two seconds later I'm back out in the crushing sun, but the brightness doesn't bother me now. Wheels down, I barely touch the ground, and I can almost feel the tiny engines in my heels ignite. In my mind my boots have sprouted wings and I am flying.

Away.

chapter four

My luck has changed at last: Hank's car is gone when I get back to the house. Inside I make a quick detour to the kitchen, because I need food. I'm even desperate enough to eat one of Hank's nasty broccoli and barley frozen feasts.

I open the fridge and, oh my God, he *did* pack me a lunch. It's in a paper bag, not a lunch box, but it does have "Delaney" written on it in Magic Marker. He must've forgotten to give it to me, or been too embarrassed to. I dump the contents out on the counter: a neatly wrapped PB&J, crustless, cut on the diagonal, a bag of mini-carrots and a box of raisins. It's a kiddie culinary cliché, but I'm starving, so I dig in.

I finish the last of the sandwich on my way down the hall to Hank's office. The door is closed—and locked. This is no big deal. We had the same locks at our apartment in New Jersey. I accidentally locked the bathroom door on my way out once, and Mom showed me how to break back in. All you need is something long and pointy, like an ice pick or a screwdriver, to shove into the little hole in the middle of the knob and pop the button lock. After last night's exploration, I know exactly where to look. I grab a couple of the letter openers from the living room, and a fountain pen in case the letter openers are too big.

The first letter opener fits, though, and I wiggle it until I feel the tip catch on the spring for the lock. The door opens and I'm in. I sit down in front of the desk and tug on the bottom drawer until it's out a sliver, then use the fat side of the letter opener as a crowbar, forcing the drawer out far enough for me to slip my fingers in and press down on the stuff inside. A couple of hard yanks and the drawer jerks open.

It's not hundred-dollar bills inside, though. Instead the drawer is crammed with photos and cards and goofy kid drawings. Confusion, surprise and disbelief jumble together in my head as I recognize that they're all of me, from me, by me.

I dump a big handful onto my lap. My eyes are instantly drawn to a greeting card near the top. "Happy Father's Day," it reads, and inside, "From your favorite daughter." On the left side, written with a pink glitter pen: "Dear

Daddy, How are you I am fine. We got a new swing set. I miss you. I love you. XOXO Delaney."

Next is a photo, a digital snap printed on regular paper, its ink so faded that the only colors are purple and pink. In it, I'm waving cheerfully at the camera and wearing the dress Mom got me for my seventh-birthday party. My princess costume.

I remember that day, but I remember it like a picture of someone else. A storybook character or a little girl from a movie. My younger self smiles up at me. I can't recall what it feels like to be so joyful. To have hope and believe in happily-ever-after.

Suddenly I want to see it all. I scoop everything out of the drawer and spread it out on the floor. Using postmarks and photo date stamps and guesses, I shift items into chronological order. There's nothing of me from when I was a baby. In the earliest pictures I can find, I'm already standing, two years old at least. There are lots of me with Mom through the years, a few with Hank, and even a couple with all of us together. Mom seems really happy, not heartbroken or tense. Hank's the one who looks sad and left out, like a kid at a party who's only there because the birthday boy was forced by his parents to invite him.

Laid out in a row, with the letters from the same year stacked on top of each other, the papers are like a skateboard ramp, or one of those cartoon drawings of a snake that's swallowed a dog or monkey—big in the middle, tapering off on both ends. The years I was nine and ten, it seems like I wrote every week. The letters were always the same cheerful reports of the nothing stuff I was doing and the final wish: "See you soon!"

Blinks of memory come back. Getting Mom to buy me special stationery, with daisies on the bottom or stars along the edge. Using different-color pens for each sentence, so the paragraphs looked like horizontal rainbows. Peeling off my favorite stickers to seal the envelopes.

Though the words are the same in a lot of the letters, I can decode the slowly dying hope of seeing Hank again, or of even getting a letter back from him. It's like reading a book about a girl who doesn't know about the bad stuff that's coming, but you do, and so you're crushed way before she is.

If I had ever laid out the cards he sent *me* on random birthdays and holidays, it would be a short trail, with a tiny hill in the middle. A baby garter snake that swallowed a crayon. Not that I could do it, because I tossed them out forever ago, with my other kiddie toys and baby dreams.

What I can't figure out is why Hank has kept this stuff. Then I remind myself that he crammed it all in a bottom drawer, out of sight.

I hear the front door open, and this time I don't dash to my room and hide. I lean back on my hands and listen as I picture Hank going into the kitchen, seeing the scraps from my bag lunch, and looking around in confusion—or maybe irritation? A few seconds and then here he comes, down the hall, almost passing by the office before catching sight of me on the floor, surrounded by the contents of his secret stash.

"What's going on? Why aren't you in school?"

Instead of answering, I hold out a handful of the letters and photos and ask a question of my own: "Why did you keep these?"

Hank stands there and about a million years go by until, at last, he says, "Why wouldn't I? You're my *daughter*." He tries to make it sound like I'm an idiot for asking, but it comes out like a bank robber saying "I'm innocent" when he's got a bag of stolen cash in his hand.

The letters flutter pathetically as I wave the pile at him. "You never wrote back. You barely even answered my emails," I say. "You stopped coming to see me. You never wanted to see me when you did come. So why . . ." My voice has gotten creaky and I worry that I sound like I still care, which I don't. That was another me, the un-wised-up me. To prove it doesn't bother me, I toss the stuff back onto the floor like the trash that it is. Hank flinches as if I've thrown it at him.

"I *did* want to see you, Delaney . . ." It seems like he's going to say something else, but instead he sits down in the desk chair and leans over to pick up one of the photos.

"But . . . ?"

Hank stares at the picture and I wonder if he's trying to remember the girl I was too, or if to him it's more like looking at someone who was always a stranger. He gently sets the photo back on the pile and rests his hands on his knees. His gaze shifts to the shelves and his eyes narrow a little, like he's trying to psychically extract advice from one of his books.

"It was difficult. My job is . . . all-consuming."

"Yeah, I know. You told me. Twenty-four/seven."

"And you lived so far away. Plus, I don't think your mom really wanted me to come."

"That's not true!" I jump up from the floor. "I used to hear her on the phone all the time, begging you to visit me. I gave up on you way before she did." My arms go stiff, the anger shooting through them to my fists. "But you gave up on me first." The room seems to have shrunk and I feel like I've got to escape quick, before the walls move in any further and trap me. I stomp to the door, my boots crushing the letters and cards and dead hopes scattered on the carpet.

Back in my room, I dive onto the bed. My eyes sting and I am so mad all I can see are sparks.

"Delaney . . ."

"Get out!" I scream, then press my face into the pillow. I crumple the bedspread in my hands, and little embroidered spirals press into my palms. I take slow breaths, concentrating on the sharp laundry-detergent smell of the pillowcase.

I feel Hank hovering at the door. "I wish . . ." His voice is quiet, wistful.

I turn my head away from him. "You wish what? That

I'd never come here? So do I." The dolls and stuffed animals on the shelves glare at me, mocking. I glare back. "Let me go home. I know you don't want me here."

Hank hesitates a second, then comes all the way in and sits down on a corner of the bed. He's so close to the edge, he'd fall off if I tapped him with my foot. I should do it—but I don't.

"I do want you here, Delaney." There's a helpless, non–Dr. Hank tone to the way he says this that makes it sound sincere, but I'm not ready to believe him yet.

I raise my head and wipe away the few tears that managed to leak out. "So that's why you ran out to see your girlfriend like a second after I got here? And then you wouldn't even admit she's your girlfriend?"

"Andrea's not my girlfriend. She's a client, like I said." Hank's phone rings. He groans. "I don't believe it. I'm sorry. I'll tell her I'll call her back."

"Why don't you just let it go to voice mail?" Hank considers this like it's some radical new idea. He sets the phone on the bed. It rings a couple more times, then stops.

Hank intertwines his fingers, then taps his chin with his thumbs. Another one of the life-coach poses I've seen before. There's something different about it this time, though. Like he really is thinking seriously and not just pretending to.

"I shouldn't have left you last night. It was the wrong thing to do. It's just that Andrea is an exceptionally hard case, and this . . ." He unclasps his hands and waves at the air between us. "It's new to me."

"How is it new? I've been on the planet for fifteen years. You blew me off at birth."

"That's not true, Delaney. Your mom moved away and never told me she was pregnant. A few years later, I was in New York promoting my first book and she saw me on TV. You'd started asking about your dad, and I guess she decided you had a right to know him, so she called me." I knew they'd broken up before I was born, but Mom would never tell me why. I learned to stop asking, because it didn't matter. I had her.

"That's the first time I met you," Hank says. "You were about two. After that, I tried to see you as much as I could."

"Lie."

"It is most certainly *not*—"

"Yeah, you came and took me to the park or the zoo or some other clichéd weekend-daddy activity. For a *while*. And then—*poof!*—you were out of there. You never even let me visit." Hank's phone rings again. "Tell her you're with another client."

"There's only Andrea."

I lean up on my elbow. "You only have *one* client?"

"One at a time."

"You must charge a lot."

Hank doesn't answer. The phone rolls over to voice mail again. He raises his eyes and finally looks at me, but his expression has changed. It's as if he's looking at someone who seems kind of familiar but who he's only just begun to recognize.

"You're right. I should've spent more time with you. If I could do it over, I'd do it differently." The phone rings *again*. No wonder he's only got one client at a time, if they're all this out-of-control. "I'll turn it off."

"No, it's okay. You can answer it." My fury has faded a little, as if the bed has absorbed it, and I'm curious about what's so urgent that this Andrea lady has to hit redial every five seconds.

"Hello, Andrea," Hank says wearily. "Mm-hmm. . . . I thought we agreed that you'd try it on your own for a few days. . . . Yes, I know, but I really think it's—" Hank listens. He leans over and presses his fingers to his forehead like he's been struck with a migraine. "Okay, Andrea. . . . I will. . . . All right." He hangs up.

"You have to go out." I say it before he can. I'm getting mad again because two seconds ago he was apologizing and trying to bond and be Mr. Paternal, but now there's no follow-through.

"I'll make it quick. As quick as I can. How about I pick up dinner on the way back?" Like drive-thru slop is going to make everything okay. "What do you want?"

"I want to come with you."

"Delaney . . ."

"I'll wait in the car. We can go out to dinner after." Here's his chance to prove that he really wants to spend

54

time with me. Plus I still have a lot of questions that need answers.

Hank gives me the look again. That "maybe I *do* know you" look. "Okay," he says.

★ ★ ★

A half hour later, we pull up in front of a small court-yard bordered by two rows of little cottage-in-the-woods-type apartments, each with its own two-step front stoop.

Hank turns off the engine and sits there a second, his hands on the wheel. "Don't worry about me," I say. "I brought a book." Hank doesn't move. Instead he glances over and studies me again. "I thought this was a life-coaching emergency," I say, hoping this will get him to stop staring. "She could be losing precious ounces of self-esteem with every second you delay. Better hurry up, Doctor, before it's too late."

Hank half smirks, sighs and finally gets out. After he closes the door, he leans in the window. "I'll be back in twenty minutes. Or less."

"Gotcha." I tap the time on my cell. "On your mark, get set, go." Another smirk, a full one this time, then he heads up the center walk into the complex. I watch and wait, although if this world-shattering therapy session is only going to take twenty minutes, I can't wait too long. Once he's out of sight, I get out of the car and look around. There's a narrow lane along one side of the complex, so I decide to try that.

Moving from apartment to apartment, I peer into

kitchens and dens, but most are dark. A TV's on in one den, but there's just an old guy inside, watching a fishing show.

"Andrea, what did I tell you—"

"I've tried, Dr. Hank. I have."

I follow the voices around to the back of the building, to a door with a spiky cactus plant in front of it, next to a recycling bin filled with cat-food tins and empty bottles of Wellness Tea. Through the slatted window beside the door, I can see a tiny bathroom cluttered with candles. A shower curtain covered in cartoon cats hangs over the tub, and inspirational messages cut out of magazines are taped to the mirror.

The bathroom door is open to the room beyond, where Hank paces back and forth, in and out of sight. A woman crosses in front of him. Andrea, I guess. "I know I'm supposed to do it on my own," she says. "But I can't even do my hair without a disaster." She's wearing an oversized T-shirt and polka-dotted sweatpants. Half of her ashy blond hair hangs straight, and the other half is screwed up in crazy, tiny curls.

"You give up too easily, Andrea. You don't try."

"I do!"

I need a better view. The path continues around to the center walk, and I enter the courtyard from the back. Andrea's front window is half hidden by bushy vines with little white flowers that give off the same perfumey scent I smelled last night and a bunch of freaky-looking plants with big leaves and blooms shaped like pointy-tufted birds. I wade into the flock but keep my head ducked down.

Inside Andrea's apartment, it's all big pillows and scarves draped over lamps and tables, and there's a cat peering out from under the couch. In the middle of the room stand Hank and Andrea. Andrea's bouncing up and down on her toes like an ecstatic kindergartner. "Oh, thank you, Dr. Hank!" Damn. I definitely missed something.

"One more night, Andrea," Hank warns. "That's all."

One more night of what? I wonder. Hank pulls a pen out of his pocket. Is he going to write her a prescription or something? Is this his secret? He's actually a drug dealer?

Instead of writing anything down, he backs up a few steps. I can't see the pen, but he lifts his arm and it looks like he's pointing it at her. There's a spark of light from somewhere and I assume it's the reflection of the sun. I glance over my shoulder, but the sun's already dropped behind the other side of the building, leaving just a pale pink sky. Huh. That's weird.

When I turn back, Andrea's gone.

No, not gone, but . . . turned into somebody else. It's her, but totally different, like she's been put through some sort of beautifying car wash. Her hair is swept up in a French twist and she's now wearing a shiny sapphire blue microminidress and matching blue kitten heels. Her eyes seem brighter and I think she may even be taller. She dashes to a mirror and squeals in delight. "Oh, Dr. Hank! This is perfect!"

I don't get it. Were there two of her? Is this a twin? If it is, where's Andrea? I shift around and try to see farther into the apartment, and I get a big bunch of the white blooms in my face. Great. If it wasn't already hard enough to see, now my eyes are watering and the scent is making me dizzy. Maybe I'm having some sort of jasmine-induced hallucination.

"You're the best fairy godmother in the world!" I hear Andrea say. What is she talking about? Is that some strange California slang term for life coach? "I'm going to text Aaron right now!"

That's when I sneeze. Loud. Andrea looks out the window and screams. When I try to back out of the bushes, I trip, and it's only by grabbing one of the huge bird-plant neck-stems that I stop myself from face-planting onto the concrete walk. Unfortunately, I decapitate a couple of the birds along the way. I couldn't help it. It was them or me.

"Delaney?" I glance up to see Hank, who's come outside and is staring down at me, half perplexed, half irritated.

Andrea—the pretty twin Andrea—steps up beside him. "Oh, is this your daughter?" She holds out her hand to me. "It's so great to meet you!" She's over her scare and now it's as if finding me in the bushes is simply another wonderful moment in her evening. I don't shake her hand so much as use it for leverage to haul myself out of the jungle. "Why didn't you come to the door?"

"I think the better question is what Delaney is doing here at all, since I asked her to wait in the car."

"It's been over twenty minutes," I say, even though I know it's been nowhere near that.

"You should've brought her in with you, Dr. Hank. She didn't need to wait outside."

"Think about that for a minute, Andrea."

"What? *Oh* . . . she doesn't know?"

I look up from plucking the last bits of sappy feather-petals off my shirt. "Know what?"

The now-familiar beat of silence between Hank and me ensues, but it's not awkward this time so much as tense. I'm getting tired of it. "Know *what*?"

"What did you see?" Hank asks calmly. Too calmly. Too "it doesn't really matter what you saw," which means it *does*.

What *did* I see, though? Nothing, really. Or nothing I can describe in a way that Hank won't brush off with some flip explanation. So I take a risk.

"*Everything.*"

Andrea's eyes pop wide and Hank's back stiffens. I hold his gaze. Showdown. Hank's eyes flick away first. I win . . . I think. Hank turns to Andrea. "Okay, Andrea. We'll do the car."

"Oh, thank you!" Andrea claps and scurries off toward the garages that line the alley behind the building, her heels click-clacking on the concrete.

"I believe you may have seen *something,* Delaney," Hank says to me as we follow Andrea to the alley. "But I doubt you understood what it was." Andrea lifts one of the garage doors, revealing a rusted tomato-red junkyard special. "I intended to put off telling you about this until after you'd settled in, but maybe it's for the best."

I really don't see what the big deal is. So he gives his clients fashion advice in addition to therapy. Why should I care? If there's some life-coach oath he's violating, I'll never tell. "I want you to pay close attention," he continues. "What you're about to see is likely to be very confusing. Your brain is going to have a hard time processing it. You'll try to come up with logic-based explanations, and you'll probably start to feel overwhelmed, even panicky. So try to relax."

Uh-huh. The only thing my brain is having a hard time processing is his monotonous, nonsensical rambling. "I'm beyond relaxed," I say. "I'm ready to fall asleep."

Andrea has managed to start the car after about fifty engine-grinding tries and has now backed out into the alley. She's bouncing again, this time on her butt instead of her heels, and not excitedly but impatiently. "Aaron might be there already, Dr. Hank," she says, a pleading whine in her voice. "He might be wondering where I am."

"Just a second, Andrea." Hank stays focused on me. "This isn't a joke, Delaney. You wanted to know what I'm doing here. I'm going to show you. But I want you to be prepared."

"Okay, okay. *Whatever.*"

Hank turns back to Andrea and takes out his pen again. This is the part I don't get. What's with the pen? "Midnight, Andrea," Hank warns. "That's how long it'll last. Like always."

"I'll be back," Andrea promises.

How long *what* lasts? What's he talking about? Hank glances up and down the alley in an "is the coast clear?" kind of way, then points his pen at the car and there's that weird spark again, but it's more like a shimmer this time—and it's coming from the pen. I look up but the sky is purple now, the sun definitely gone. When I shift my gaze to the streetlamp, to see if that's what's reflecting off the pen, a bright light flashes behind me and I blink.

Then I open my eyes.

Andrea now sits in a dark cherry-red convertible, shiny and new, right out of a car commercial. The tomato junk heap has vanished. Andrea grins, revs the motor and waves as Hank calls "Midnight!" Then she speeds down the alley to the street.

I feel woozy again, even though there's no jasmine anywhere nearby. I desperately need to see the other car, Andrea's real car, but it's gone. Did I ever see it? Am I still hallucinating? Am I even awake?

A second later, Hank shakes my arm, and my eyes open. I'm in Hank's car and we're driving. It's dark out. Streetlamps wash pools of yellow-gray light over us as we pass by them. It *was* a dream. Thank God.

"You fainted," Hank says.

"I fell asleep. What time is it? How long were you in there? It had to be way longer than twenty minutes."

"You weren't asleep, Delaney. Everything you saw happened."

"Right. I really saw Andrea call you her fairy godmother."

"I prefer not to give it a label."

This weird dread comes over me, but why? "Give *what* a label?" Nothing is making any sense.

"It's an ability, an aptitude. Like athletic skill, or a talent for art. It's inherited. It's supposed to pass from mother to daughter, but the bloodline's gotten diluted over the years and"—he gestures to himself—"this is what happened."

"So you're actually a fairy god*father*?" I laugh, but it sounds creepy in my ears. It's the laugh of a crazy person. *That's* what this is. I'm not sleeping or hallucinating. I'm going insane.

"You're disassociating, Delaney. Concentrate. Tell me what you saw. That'll help you make it concrete."

"I *dreamed* you turned Andrea into Cinderella. I *imagined* you turned her car into a carriage, a red one. No four white horses, though." I laugh again. It's definitely a cackle this time.

"It was a red Ferrari. And yes, that's what I did."

I remember the pen now, the glowing-shimmer pen. "With your magic wand."

"That's good, Delaney. You're absorbing it now." Is he crazy too? Why isn't he giving me the real story? About how light refracts and a person's focus can be redirected and the mind tricked, all with a little sleight of hand.

Aha! *That's* it! "You *hypnotized* me!" But why? Is it some bizarre life-coach therapy to treat grief? It's not working, because I don't feel better. I might even feel worse.

Hank sighs. He shakes his head. "I guess I'm going to have to show you again and prove it."

★ ★ ★

"What are we looking for?"

"Someone with a wish." Hank searches the crowd as we walk. "A small one."

We're at a mall, but like everything else out here in the land of flawless beauty, it's an alien dreamscape. It's all outdoors, for one thing, with the shops set along a curving path. The stores are two stories high, but there's nothing upstairs, just fake European balconies strung with twinkling lights.

"I'll give you a wish. Turn my boots into glass slippers."

"It doesn't work that way, Delaney. It can't be a random demand. It has to be a genuine internal desire."

We wind around outdoor vendors selling jewelry made from crystals, lotion scented with jasmine—like I need any more of *that* scent clogging up my brain—and flip-flops in every color in the universe. It's the street of endless shopping. Everything you didn't know you wanted, nothing you need.

Hank pauses in front of a fountain where curved arcs of water sway to some old jazz song. I wish I'd brought my iPod with me. At least I'd have *some* connection to reality.

"Get me my iPod from the house," I say.

"I *told* you—"

"It's a genuine wish! I just wished it. I *swear.*"

Hank ignores me and studies a little boy standing a few feet away, holding a cup of vanilla-chocolate swirl ice cream and pouting. "Aha," Hank murmurs. He pulls out his pen.

"They were out of plain vanilla, sweetie," the boy's mother says. "Just eat around the chocolate."

"But I don't *want* to." The boy's voice is choked with despair at the grand unfairness of life. Welcome to the club, kid.

Then, suddenly, the boy's misery vanishes, replaced by elation. "Mommy!" He holds up the cup and I can see that the fudge ribbons are gone. It's all vanilla.

Hank turns to me, half smug, half expectant.

Is he kidding? "You're telling me *you* did that?" Impossible. The ice cream scoop shifted to hide the chocolate, that's all. I watch the boy as he follows his mother around to the other side of the fountain and wait for him to discover the awful truth, but the little vanilla lover keeps happily eating, as if the chocolate really did disappear.

If . . .

There can't be any "if," because "if" suggests that it's possible.

"Enough time has passed for your belief system to ac-climate, Delaney. It's only your intellect that's resisting."

"Doesn't 'intellect' mean the *smart* part of my brain?"

Hank repeats his sigh from the car. "Fine. If you're going to be that way."

He proceeds to "show me," again and again. And again. Leading me in and out of stores, waving his pen, granting more wishes. A size 10 skirt appears on a rack where there had only been size 2s, and the size 10 shopper who had been combing through them smiles in delight. A woman is told by a clerk that the handbag she holds doesn't come in green, only to have it turn to a bright lemon-lime while neither is looking. A man drops his camera in the fountain, and it reappears in his hand. A toddler flings a yellow ball from his stroller, and it's back in his lap before his parents notice, before the toddler has a chance to let out a cry. Left and right, things are fixed, problems solved. In the blink of an eye.

I watch these little miracles happen, and with each one, some tiny piece of the logical part of my thinking is chipped away. I can't believe *it,* but I'm starting to believe *him.*

The pen stays the pen, though, through it all. "Why isn't the pen doing that glowy thing?"

"That doesn't happen with small wishes, only with the big ones. The ones for your clients." He actually calls them clients. I don't remember *that* from the fairy tale.

"Let me see." I take the pen and study it. I shake it. "How does it work?"

"It's not the pen. You can use any pointed object. That's how you focus your intention and direct the energy. With small wishes, it's only directed one way, from you to the recipient. But with your clients, there's a connection between you, like an electrical current. You're linked to their wishes. The energy this creates charges the pen, or whatever you're using, and the pen becomes—"

"A magic wand."

" 'Magic' is a word people use when they don't know how to explain something," Hank says. "That makes it sound supernatural, but it's a perfectly natural physical process. You're not creating something from nothing. You're manipulating what's already there."

"So you can, like, read all these people's minds?"

"I can't read anyone's mind. For small wishes, you're guessing what they want, in that moment, from observing them. But with your client, because of the bond you have with them, you . . . feel their yearning, and the feeling doesn't go away until you've granted their wish."

I point the pen at him. "So this is your big secret. The reason you left Mom, right? You didn't want her to know."

Hank takes the pen out of my hand. "That *is* why our relationship ended. But it's not because she didn't know."

"That doesn't make any sense."

"She didn't like that I was always running off to help a client. She thought it meant I didn't care enough about her. As if I had a choice." He pockets the pen. "She wanted me to quit, but that's like asking someone to quit being half Irish. It's not something you can change."

"I don't believe you. She wasn't like that. Plus she would've told me."

"She wanted to protect you."

"From *what*?" Hank doesn't answer. I try to come up with proof that he's making it all up, but my brain has hit information overload.

A trio of kindergartners run onto the lawn behind the fountain, waving those toxic neon glow-in-the-dark sticks, chasing each other around and shrieking. It's one quasi-magic wand too many, and a bunch of images suddenly hit me at once, banging together like scenes from a frenzied music video. Mom in the hospital, the stacks of photos and letters in Hank's desk, Andrea in her dress and in her car, and flashes of light. Over and over, they speed past in my head. It's all too much.

"I'm sorry, Delaney. This is a lot of emotionally intensive information for you to have to take in all at once." If he really cared about me, he'd stop the Dr. Hank pseudo-science crap, because that's making my brain swirl even more. "We should sit down." Hank guides me over the tiny toy bridge toward a small bench beside a brass statue of a little boy and his dog, frozen in a state of carefree joy. I never thought I'd be jealous of a piece of metal.

I don't want to sit down. I want to get away.

Ding ding. The trolley that takes awed tourists, excited

kids and lazy shoppers from one end of the mall to the other grinds up its track at one one-hundredth of a mile per hour. Hank steps aside to let it pass, but I dart across the tracks so it separates us.

I shake the images crowding my head loose and text Posh: "Mental Health Emergency." No response. The time on the screen is 8:15 p.m. That's 11:15 New Jersey time. *Star Trek* reruns on Syfy. Why is she always out in geekland when I'm in a crisis?

There's a department store ahead. It's the closest thing to an escape I can find, so I cut in front of a man opening the door for his wife and slip inside.

I hate department stores, with their crisscrossing escalators, hairless cardboard-colored mannequins, piped-in piano music and women with pinched faces, as if the shopping bags hanging from their elbows are a cruel burden they've been forced to bear. I especially hate the shoe departments, because they're always filled with too many stupid styles that you *know* will be on the sale rack tomorrow so why did they even bother, and fashion crimes like leopard-print sandals and ballet slippers with plastic roses safety-pinned to the toe.

The boots are no better. There are the usual red cowboy boots and slouchy suede ankle boots in lollipop colors like orange and grape, and Uggs in all sizes. Nothing I would be caught dead—or alive—wearing. The display shoes are always size 6, which is my size, so I grab a pair of basic black calf-length boots and put them on.

I hate them. The toe's too tight and the calf's too loose and the zipper scratches. The heel is skinny and wobbly and the black is boring. I want to scream, I hate them so much.

I'm definitely feeling more like myself again.

"Those are fantastic." One of the shoe salesmen is standing behind me and pointing to my boots on the floor. I'd changed into my dragon boots before we went to Andrea's. The body and tail are painted up the sides, and one's tipped over, so you can see the fiery open mouth carved onto the sole. I pick it up. The worn leather is soft in my hand, the chunky heel reassuringly heavy.

"Thanks."

"Where did you get them?"

"They're originals. Custom-made."

"I should've guessed." He shifts into work mode, gesturing to the boots I have on. "And how are you liking those?"

"Not so much."

He nods, with a little "I didn't think so" smile. "Well, let me know if you need any help." He leaves to wait on real customers. When I put my boots back on, they're so comfortable and perfect, they're like a hug. I admire them in a floor mirror. They *are* fantastic.

My mind is calm again. Clear. So clear that a thought occurs to me. Something that I can't believe I didn't think of before. Or maybe I did, but I guess I needed to "process it" too.

"Delaney?" Hank makes his way through stacks of shoe boxes and clusters of shoe shoppers toward me. "What are you doing in here? You can't just run off like that." He waits for a response, his scolding look morphing into worry.

Why am I having so much trouble speaking? It's five words. But they're taking up all the space in my mind—all that precious space I had cleared out. The words are huge, that's why. Just when I think they're too big to ever make it out, I say them:

"I'm a fairy godmother too."

"No." Hank's eyes dart around, but no one's paying attention. Trying on shoes is one of those all-consuming tasks. You really don't have time to notice fathers and daughters discussing their supernatural genetic makeup.

"You said it was hereditary."

"I also said it passed from mother to daughter," Hank says in a hushed voice. "I'm not your mother."

"*You're* not a daughter either."

"Let's discuss this somewhere else, all right?"

I glare at him, toss the black boots back on the shelf and then march past him, zigzagging through the slip-on sneakers and lace-up wedges to the handbag section. Hank tries to catch up but he's no good at navigating sales racks and discount tables. Not my problem. I spot a door on the other side of the coat department and head for it.

"Delaney—"

I pause as a new thought occurs to me. One that makes

me want to grab a tasseled two-toned scarf off a nearby rack and strangle Hank with it.

I spin around to face him. "How could you not have told me this? I could've been using my powers this whole time! I could've helped Mom."

"No, you couldn't. You can't change reality, only alter bits of it."

"I could've *tried*." I turn my back on him, push open the door and step out.

"It doesn't matter anyway, because you're not—"

I let the door close on him and look around. I'm back outside but in a different area than where I came in. Ahead is a row of mini-restaurants—Greek, Italian, Mexican, French, a mix-and-match play dining set.

Hank appears next to me, so I start moving again. "I've watched you over the years, Delaney. Very carefully. You never showed any signs."

"Watched me *when?* In the five half-hour visits you've made in the whole fifteen years of my life?"

"There were more than five. And they were more than a half-hour long."

"They weren't enough for you to know *anything* about me."

"*You'd* know."

At the far end of restaurant row is a normal-sized diner. Finally, something real. Hank probably thinks I'm slowing down because I'm listening to him, but it's really because suddenly I'm starving. I've probably been hungry all along, but my brain's been too busy to pay attention to my body. A bowl of cereal, a mini-bag of pretzels and a kindergartner's lunch is not enough calories to fuel the day I've had so far. I need food right now. Comfort food.

I'm already at the diner door when Hank says, "Good idea. Let's get something to eat," like it was his idea, but whatever. I'm too weak from hunger to correct him.

Of course, the diner turns out to be nothing like the ripped-vinyl, cracked-linoleum places back in New Jersey. The booths here are eye-popping purple. The waitresses are TV-star pretty and Cadie Perez–friendly, and the tiny individual jukeboxes are plastic facades covering speakers that spray identical fifties tunes out over each table.

At least the food is familiar. I order my favorite: grilled cheese and tomato with mayo and a side of fries. But once the food comes, my stomach clenches up. I stuff the fries down one by one, but they just lie there in greasy lumps in my chest. It would be nice if I could let go of my rage for five minutes so I could enjoy one meal today, but this is impossible, since the cause of the rage is sitting across from me, calmly eating his fruit salad as if my entire understanding of how the world works hasn't just been shattered into a million mismatched pieces.

Hank stabs a piece of pineapple, pops it in his mouth and then points the fork toward a revolving display case of sliced pie. "You *do* have cherry," a man who'd been studying the pies says a second later. In the booth across from us, a lady shakes her almost-empty ketchup bottle and

Hank waves the fork her way, refilling it. The lady blinks in surprise as ketchup pours out.

"Stop *doing* that." He's not "showing me" anymore, he's showing *off*.

"I'm glad you're finally talking to me." Hank smiles and spears a tangerine slice. I don't answer. Instead I stuff in another fry and try not to gag. "You shouldn't feel bad that the ability didn't pass down to you, Delaney. You're better off."

"Who said I feel bad?" I'm relieved. I am. Why would I want to be a freak like Hank? Still, it's one more thing I can't have. One more thing I don't get a choice about.

"It doesn't surprise me, really," he says. "The DNA's been so diluted over the centuries—we had to die out eventually."

"You mean there aren't any others? You're it?"

"As far as I know. Although I've wondered sometimes about people who are overly empathetic. The ones who are always rescuing dogs and feeding the homeless. I suspect they might be distant descendants."

"That's what Mom wanted to protect me from, right? Being one too."

Hank sets down his fork and leans back. "I warned her early on that you might have inherited the powers, but since she believed it was something I chose to do, not *had* to do, she didn't want me giving you 'ideas.' She made me promise not to tell you."

"That's why you never asked me to come visit. Because

you decided it was better for me to think you hated me than for you to tell me the truth."

Hank meets my eyes, which is brave, because if I could shoot laser beams out of them, he'd be ashes. "I wish now I'd fought harder to tell you, Delaney. I always imagined that on my next trip to see you I *would* tell you, no matter what. But it never seemed like the right time, so I kept putting it off. . . ." My laser-beam stare must get to him, because he looks away.

My whole life, I've had all these questions. I wish somebody had told me before I asked them that I wouldn't like *any* of the answers.

★ ★ ★

In bed that night, I can't get to sleep. I've got way too much to digest, food-wise *and* thought-wise. I stare up at the earrings I've dangled through the little eyelet holes in the lace canopy. I don't wear earrings. They're Mom's. Something easy to bring with me. They twinkle in the light from the Snow White lamp, and it feels like Mom is smiling down at me, but from really, really far away. Too far away to talk to her. Too far away for her to hear me.

I still can't believe she knew all this and kept it from me. Whenever I got upset about not seeing Hank, she'd always cheer me up by saying we didn't need anybody but each other. I believed that, but now I see that my knowing about Hank being an f.g., and my possibly being one too, would've meant more time spent with Hank and less with her, and this would've broken up our tight one-on-

one world. But why didn't she tell me at the end, when she had to know I would find out? Did she think I'd be mad? Was she worried she would lose me?

I wish Mom were here so I could ask her. I wish Posh would remember to check her messages and call me back. I wish I could figure out what's true and what's not. I wish *I* had a fairy godmother to grant some of these wishes for me.

And I wish I knew if I was one . . .

Because what I didn't tell Hank is that when I was little, I used to think I could make good things happen for people. I did it all the time, even for strangers. I'd sort of imagine something and it would come true. Mom used to say I was a good-luck charm. Later I realized it was a bunch of coincidences. If I were a good-luck charm, Mom would still be here.

But now, I don't know. I don't know anything anymore. My brain feels like it's run a marathon and wants to collapse already. I let it zone out, but my eyes stay open, still looking up at Mom's earrings for answers. After today, I wouldn't be surprised if they *did* start talking, spouting advice through little pin-sized mouths in tiny tinny voices. Then the frog prince alarm clock and the Tinker Bell night-light will join in, and soon every object in the room will have gone all enchanted and magical.

Except me.

chapter five

"... In a chemical reaction, substances are changed into other substances. ..."

Mr. McElroy's up at the front of the class lecturing. Thank God there's no lab today, so I don't have to pay attention. My thoughts are all jumbled, like I put my brain on backward this morning.

More weird dreams last night, this time involving lots of twinkling lights and feathery wings and me in this horrific wedding cake of a dress, with boots made of glass. They magnified my toes, which was not pretty, and I don't remember how they felt, but they couldn't have been comfortable.

Posh woke me out of my dream, calling my cell at predawn Pacific standard time. "Sorry!" she squealed. "I forgot about the time difference!" While I worked on achieving full consciousness, she gave me a rundown of the new examples of symbolism she'd found in *The Golden Compass,* after reading it last night for the thirtieth time.

I debated whether I should tell her about Hank and his Grimm brothers secret, and the need to just *say* it, to make it concrete with words, won out. When she finally paused for breath, I quickly jumped in and told her everything, from finding the letters, to Andrea's dress. From the chocolate-swirl ice cream to the refilled ketchup bottle.

"Wow! That is so cool! It's like you're living in a graphic novel." Just like that, she accepted it. Ms. Science. Of course, she's also Ms. Science Fiction.

"You don't think there's some other, rational explanation?"

"It sounds rational to me." She told me she'd seen this documentary on the Paranormal Channel about how there are people who've been scientifically proven to have unusually high levels of intuition, which translates as ESP. "And last week I read an article on the-psychic-report-dot-com that said you can train yourself to be telekinetic." She'd tried to do it herself, but you have to sit still and focus for like eight hours—about seven hours and fifty-nine minutes over Posh's limit. "Your dad is so lucky! He can extrasensory-perceive *and* telekinet. Or telekiness. Or whatever the verb is. Hold on, I'll look it up."

There it was. My new reality, officially approved by Posh. I had no choice but to accept that I was truly the daughter of a fairy godfather.

What Posh refused to believe was that I hadn't inherited the f.g. gene. Despite my moment of doubt before I fell asleep last night, and my French-fry-fueled dreams, this was the one thing I knew for a fact: I am so *not* the fairy godmother type.

"But you *have* to be one, Delaney. It doesn't make sense otherwise." Great. Now I was living in a world where being a fairy-tale creature with the power to grant wishes was more logical than *not* being one.

"I have no idea how to turn pumpkins into carriages, Posh. Or mice into horses. I don't know what anybody's wish is, and I don't care."

"Maybe the ability's atrophied, from lack of use."

"Whatever. It's not there."

"You have to find out for sure. It's your scientific and spiritual duty." Then I had to hear her sermon about how "all living things are obligated to fulfill the destiny imbued in them by Nature." This was like when they decided to give away goldfish at the school fair freshman year and Posh launched this big protest, because Nature had not intended fish to be put on display in plastic bags and then transferred to glass prisons. She guilted her father into building an actual freshwater pond in their backyard for all the goldfish to live in. After the fish died, within like two weeks, the pond fulfilled *its* destiny by being con-creted over and made into a pool.

Before I hung up, I made Posh swear not to tell her mom about Hank's big secret. Hank would deny it, and her parents wouldn't believe it anyway, so it'd be *me* who ended up looking crazy and desperate. In return, Posh made me promise that I would find out if I had the f.g. DNA after all. I said I'd try, but I already know that Nature has given me a pass. I'll let a couple of days go by and then tell her the answer is no.

". . . one compound into another. You can't change an element, however—that can only be done by a nuclear re-action. . . ."

So why am I still thinking about it? Why do all these annoying questions keep popping up in my head? "*Am* I one?" "*Should* I try to find out?" "What happens if the answer is yes?"

". . . you need to supply 'activation' energy to start the reaction. . . ."

Maybe sketching will get my mind off it. I reach into my backpack for my charcoal pencil, but it's not there. As I search through the pockets, I feel a tap on my arm. It's Flynn, at the desk next to me. He nods to the front of the room, where Mr. McElroy waits, one eyebrow raised. "I don't think you'll find the answer in there, Ms. Collins." How did he know I was looking for answers? Don't tell me Mr. McElroy's a fairy godfather too. I can't take my life getting any more bizarre. "I'll repeat the question: In an endothermic reaction, is heat given off or absorbed?"

Oh thank God, he's just talking about chemistry. Not that I care about endothermic anything. I have bigger issues on my mind. I might as well take a guess, though, since I have a fifty-fifty chance. "Absorbed."

Both of Mr. McElroy's eyebrows go up, then settle back down in nonexpression mode. "That's correct." Mr. McElroy goes back to colliding reactants and breaking atom bonds, so I'm free to finish the flying boots from yesterday. I guess I'll have to sketch in pen for now. It's not ideal, but I can always start over later. As I add feathers to the wings, the boots start to look familiar. Oh no—they're the wings from my dream. Forget it. I slash a big X through the whole page.

"Since there are no volunteers, why don't you demonstrate for us, Ms. Collins?" Great. The harassment hasn't ended. It's not fair that I'm constantly singled out like this. Flynn shrugs like "I tried." How did he try? *He* could've volunteered.

On my way to the front of the room, I glance at the board to see if I can figure out what the experiment *is* exactly. I'm trying to remember anything Mr. McElroy has said, but all I can summon up are random phrases like "double displacement" and "kinetic energy."

"This is the active yeast I mixed with warm water." He hands me a beaker. "That's the catalyst. Now add it to the hydrogen peroxide." It better not explode in my face and kill me. Although if it does, all my f.g. problems will be resolved. I pour the yeast into a big glass bowl on the front lab table. It instantly starts to bubble. "There you go. Oxygen forms on the surface and is released, leaving water. The yeast has sped up the decomposition of the hydrogen peroxide, but the yeast remains unchanged. So what have we learned here, Ms. Collins?"

"Don't try this at home?" I get a few laughs, but I know they're laughing *at* me, not with me.

"Amusing but wrong, on two levels. One: you *can* try this at home. Two: the lesson is that a catalyst can speed up a chemical reaction, as can other factors such as . . ." Mr. McElroy waves at the class to answer, and a few kids call out: "Temperature." "Concentration." "Pressure." Magic wands, I think. I could say this, as a joke, although no one would get it and there'd be no laughs this time, only stares. Posh would get it, but she wouldn't laugh either. She'd nod seriously and launch into some Harvard-genius-type speech about how this proves her right and how everything Hank's told me and shown me is not only rational but provable. Ergo, equals, therefore: I am a fairy godmother.

But I'm not. I'm *not*.

★ ★ ★

I'm not going to think about it anymore. I'm going to concentrate on school. I'm going to listen as Madame Kessler batters us with examples of the conditional tense for reflexive verbs in her clipped nasal voice. *"On se demanderait."* One would wonder.

I *do* wonder. *Je me demande* what it would be like if I did have magic powers. To make things appear, change, disappear. My life wouldn't be ruled by everyone else. *I'd* be in control for once. Instead of treating me like a freak, the Happy High students would gaze at me in awe. That might make life semibearable until I can get home to New Jersey. There'd probably be a way I could speed that up too and make Posh's parents let me go back now. I could wave my wand and a new wing would appear on the side of their house, for instance, with a bedroom for me, decorated my way. Posh wants me to come back, so it would qualify as a wish.

Things would change at East Lombard too. The kids would line up to tell me their wishes. Posh and I wouldn't have to eat at the outcast table. I'd be popular.

If I were an f.g., which I'm not. Still, Posh is going to keep bugging me about it until I prove it's not true, so what I have to do is try a small wish, really try, and fail. Then she'll get off my back, and I can let it go.

I glance around the room, but I can't find anyone in need of wish granting. The twinsetted French snobs are beyond smug in their overpriced clothes and celebrity-endorsed makeup, blessed by tutor-guided straight As and neatly arranged future plans for private college, sorority queendom and glamorous starter jobs in Los Angeles or New York. The rest of the class appears just as disgustingly content. No one even seems to want class to end early, despite the fact that Madame K's voice should be declared a crime against humanity. Her own nose scrunches up in disgust below her unibrow as she speaks, and she bites down on every word as if she wants to chop them all into bloody bits. *"Nous nous coifferions."* The high pitch of her squawking is so painful it could send a pack of wolves fleeing in aural agony.

Je me demande what makes her so stratospherically miserable. Part of it has got to be that she's bitter over being so evil-hag-looking. Ergo, equals, therefore: she wishes she were prettier.

Where to start, though, and how? I don't want to stare at her, so I'll sketch her, although I still can't find my charcoal pencil. I checked my locker between classes, but it wasn't there either. Using pen isn't the only challenge. Madame K's also moving now, going up and down the rows, ordering random victims to conjugate "to wash" and "to hurry." Her face sears the brain, though, so I do a pretty good job working off memory, capturing the scowl and the sunken eyes and the big thick single eyebrow. Since I can't erase, I put my thumb in the middle of her sketched forehead, dividing her brow in two. Wow, that makes it a lot better. Now she just looks pissy, not horrific.

Okay, so if Hank can make fudge swirls disappear from ice cream, and if I *do* have the power, I should be able to point my pen and pluck a few—

"Danielle!" Madame K's assigned French name for me pierces my eardrums with the force of a nuclear missile. *"Qu'est-ce que vous faites?"*

"Um . . ." Semideafness has switched off all my other brain functions. She snatches the notebook off my desk. *"Je ne suis pas heureuse, Danielle. Je ne suis pas du tout heureuse."* Her eyes squint down at me, her unibrow curling up like an inching caterpillar. I was *so* wrong. She's not miserable at all—*du tout*. She loves being the bitter, scary crone. *Je me demande* if she's considered a job as a cartoon villainess.

Madame K flips the sketchbook closed, preventing the kids around me who've been craning their necks from seeing what I drew. She flicks the book under her arm, clamping it between her elbow and hip, claiming it. Panic brings back my power of speech. "But that's got all of my—"

"EN FRANÇAIS!"

"Uh, *mais le cahiers ont,* I mean, *a tous mes . . ."* Clearly my power of *French* speech has fled. *"Il est les autres . . .* uh, *drawings de moins—"*

Madame K purses her gray lips in mock sympathy. *"Alors. Je regrette. C'est trop mal. Trop, trop, trop mal . . . pour* vous."

This is so unfair! All my new boot designs are in there. I need that sketchbook. *"Mais . . ."*

Now her lips go as thin as her voice. *"Bien."* She opens the notebook and viciously rips a couple of blank pages out, and the kids around me flinch. There's a spark of glee in her eyes. It's probably exactly how she looks when she's tearing the limbs off stray kittens and boiling puppies for stew.

Madame K, sketchbook assassin, hands me the ripped pages, the tiny bits of paper where the spiral held them hanging by microscopic threads. She's probably disappointed there's no dripping blood. She tells me, *en français,* of course, to use the pages to write a five-hundred-word essay on the benefits of learning French, and to complete all of the questions in Chapters *Six à Neuf,* even though we're only up to Chapter *Cinq.*

I'd rather use my pen to magically give her a beard to go with the unibrow. That's got to be her *real* wish, right? To be even more terrifying and repulsive? I'd try it, but I don't want to do anything that has even a one percent chance of making her happy.

After class, I decide to test Principal Lee's open-door policy. The door *is* open and he invites me in, but when I tell him what happened, he doesn't see my side at all.

"I'll tell you what I'd do, Delaney. I'd throw myself one hundred and fifteen percent into that assignment, be the top best A-one French student in the class from now on, and then *maybe* Mrs. Kessler will let you have the notebook back at the end of the semester. An apology wouldn't do any damage either. I always say, you can catch more flies with agave syrup than balsamic vinegar." He chuckles at his culinary non-humor.

I was trying to help *her,* I want to tell him, but of course I can't, because then I'd have to explain how, and why. The visit is an absolute complete top best A-one waste of time, other than learning that Principal Lee is not my pal after all.

Now I *really* need to know if the whole f.g. thing is true. It's not just curiosity anymore. If the power is there, I have to find it so I can get my sketchbook back. It doesn't matter that it's *my* wish. Later I can figure out how to trick somebody into wishing it for me. That'll be easy. The hard part is finding an opportunity to truly test myself.

World history is a write-off. I've got a chair now, but all the tables are full, so instead of cramming me in somewhere, Ms. Lammers sticks the new girl way in the back of the room, at a paint-covered folding table that looks like it was borrowed from some third-grade art class. The table's kind of cool, though, and anyway, who wants to be wedged in with a bunch of hostile strangers?

I'm so far back, I'm practically in South America, so I decide to check my messages. Posh has sent me links to the telekinesis article she told me about, plus a clip from the documentary. Being Posh, she's also texted me a marathon Posh-ipedia compilation of all the online info she could find. There's a report on a mind-reading experiment that was done at Berkeley in 1975, and a *Modern Psychology* article about the power of wishful thinking (which I really don't think is the same thing as granting wishes), and who knows what else, because I'm only halfway through reading about fairy sightings in the Scottish Highlands when Ms. Lammers appears next to me. What is with the teachers at this school sneaking up on people? And taking their stuff? Ms. Lammers holds out her hand, and I know she wants me to give her the phone. I don't even bother to play dumb or protest or claim an emergency. I just give it to her and mentally add it to the list of the things I need to get back.

I cheer up when I get to trig, because I know this is going to be the class where I make it happen. It's math. It's where things are proven to be true or false with no in between. Where things add up. If Hank = f.g., then Delaney + f.g. gene + determination = f.g. While Mr. Nisonson goes on about the Law of Sines, I *really* look this time, peering around the room, squinting hard at the faces, trying to read people's minds, figure out what they want. Somebody must want *something*. Even if it's just a snack. After all, it's almost lunchtime.

My eyes land on one of the guys who was sitting with Flynn at lunch. He's wearing a Marilyn Manson T-shirt and he's got the shaggy boy bangs—the angled mop that covers their eyes so they have to constantly shake their heads to see and you're always waiting for them to jerk it too far or too fast, causing them to sever a neck muscle. He's trying to use the edge of a piece of paper to draw a straight line for the scalene triangle Mr. Nisonson wrote on the board, but Shaggy keeps having to erase and start over because the paper moves or bends, causing his pencil to slip. He either forgot his ruler, or lost it, or never had one at all because he decided his school supply allowance was better spent on metal band decals for his notebook.

I point my pen his way. I concentrate. I think, *Ruler, ruler, ruler.*

Nothing happens. Maybe I need to visualize it. I close my eyes and picture a ruler and then picture it in Shaggy Boy's hand. I open my eyes and point the pen and try again, try to really feel the f.g. energy flowing through me.

Still no ruler.

I squeeze the pen, so tightly it's on the verge of snapping. I focus. Hard. I tense up, putting everything I have into it. I'm not even breathing anymore.

"Are you feeling all right, Delaney?" Every solitary head in the room turns as Mr. Nisonson says this. I'm no longer visualizing the ruler. I'm visualizing myself—what I look like clenching the pen and clenching my teeth with a constipated grimace as if those aren't the only things I'm clenching.

Then I visualize the entire class erupting in hooting, deafening, comedy-festival-crowd-sized laughter. It doesn't happen, but I can feel *that* energy for sure—energy that comes from a room full of people trying hard *not* to burst into hysterics.

"I'm fine," I say, and make it sound like there's nothing wrong at all, when really, everything is wrong.

I'm done. Problem solved. Delaney Collins ≠ f.g.

★ ★ ★

I try to cheer myself up as I head for lunch. Okay, so I'm not destined to flit around granting wishes with a magic pen. Weight off! No need to spend my life helping people. What a tedious, thankless loser life *that* would be. Hank's life, basically.

Yet it also means I have nothing to look forward to now but the same miserable day-in, day-out real life. Boring. Depressing. Normal.

Maybe "normal" isn't the right word. Not here at Happy High. The food in the lunchroom, for instance. No heat-lamped doughy pizza, no crusted-over casseroles for this crowd. It's all creepily beautiful and Technicolor. The mac and cheese is smooth and silky and the color of sunshine. The pizzas are like paintings in a modern art museum, with flecks of sun-dried tomatoes, designer mushrooms and olives that are probably flown in every morning direct from Greece. Even the nachos look like sculpture, each plate topped with a perfectly rounded ice cream scoop of guacamole.

Today's special is lemon pepper rotelle with artichoke hearts and fire-roasted tomatoes. I slide the plate onto my tray, because it's not like the other options are any less weird. Cadie and Mia, ahead of me in line, each pick one of the designer salads. Cadie's has weird fruits on it I've never seen before in my life, and Mia's actually has flowers sprinkled on top.

"Make sure you get the apple pie!" Cadie says, looking my way. I glance around, but she's definitely talking to me. "Chesley Kang's mother owns this pastry shop in Gardenia Village and she brings in like a case of them once a month. They go super fast."

"Thanks for the tip."

"Oh! Lana Francis got the last piece. Darn." Cadie

smiles at me apologetically and I don't bother to tell her I'm really not that broken up because if it doesn't have chocolate in it, forget it.

Cadie waits for me as I pay and then walks with me out the sliding glass doors. Mia's ahead, casting unhappy looks over her shoulder as Cadie and I somehow end up together at the cheerleaders' tables. My resistance must be low from the strain of the day, and I find myself sitting down in the very chair I avoided yesterday, right at the crack where the two round tables have been pushed together.

Cadie sits at the top of the figure eight, with Mia. Her table is obviously the first string. The hair of the girls there is just a pinch glossier, their skin smoother, their shoulders broader than the girls at the table on the other side of me, who strain to be included in the star table's conversation about whether silver lip gloss is a do or don't. Eventually, B-Team settles down into their own chat, dissecting one girl's date with some boy named Jonas or Jonah, or maybe Josh. It's hard to tell, since they all talk at once in the same squealy, excited voice.

I'm stuck in the vortex between two whirling, intelligence-free conversations, but at least I'm ignored by both sides and left alone. With nothing to do but think, I make a mental list of everything I've lost today: charcoal pencil, sketchbook, cell phone, dignity, self-esteem, hope. It's like a tragic poem. I swear I have enough material in my life to be a modern Elizabeth Barrett Browning.

This reminds me that in a weak moment near the end

of Brit lit yesterday, I lent my charcoal pencil to the girl in front of me, whose pen had run out, and I forgot to get it back in my rush to leave. The brain-blitzing events of last night completely buried the memory of it until now. But it wasn't only poetry that sparked the realization. It was also the cheerleader sitting next to me, at table two: the girlfriend of Jonah/Jonas/Josh. She's the one who borrowed it.

"Hey, do you have my pencil?" I ask her, interrupting an argument over whether J-guy asking her to buy the popcorn for the movie was a bad sign. She looks at me like not only do I smell (which I do *not*), not only am I an unforgivably offensive presence at the table (which I already *know*), but it is also stratospherically beyond outrageous that I should ask her to return something that she deigned to lower herself to borrow in the first place, and I should consider it a gift to her and be grateful she had the generosity to accept it.

Too bad she's mistaken me for one of those members of the lower castes that can be intimidated by queenly scorn. I don't say anything. I don't change expression. I just wait. She finally lets out a huff and her fellow date dissectors roll their eyes in support. She digs though her leather book bag—probably made from sacred Indian cows—and retrieves my pencil.

"Thank you," I say sweetly. I can feel her loathing through the pencil as she hands it to me—and this flips another switch in my head, causing bits and pieces of today to come back to me. Stuff I hadn't paid attention to but that had slipped into my brain anyway. Energy creates a reaction. Compounds break apart and reassemble into something new. Complementary angles add up.

I can't keep the thoughts straight. They're jumbled together and firing off in different directions. Then more memories come, mixing in with the others. I wonder if this is how Posh's brain is all the time. No wonder she can never relax and be quiet. She's got to get the ideas *out*.

So do I, but my way. I take out the blank pages Madame K ripped from my sketchbook and write "apple + butter + sugar + flour = apple pie." I sketch a slice of pie and draw an arrow from the words to the image. Okay, now what? It's still not fitting together.

I take a break from thinking to draw in a scoop of ice cream next to the pie—and then it hits me. There was no ice cream, and now there is. It started in my mind and now it's on the page, thanks to the pencil. Some people might call that magic. But it's really just the result of a combination of elements: charcoal dust and paper. Plus thought. My thought. The "activation energy."

It can't be that easy. Can it? Wouldn't anybody be able to do it?

But I'm not anybody.

I point the pencil toward Cadie's plate. The ingredients come together in my mind, as if I'm going to draw the pie, and I send the idea down my arm to the pencil, and then to the plate. I'm calm and confident. Cadie is going to get the slice of apple pie she wished for. . . .

Not even an apple seed.

Lunch ends. Cadie stands and picks up her empty, apple pie–free plate, signaling her minions. They rise and follow her back into the school, leaving me at the crack between the two tables, alone with my failure.

"Uch!"

"Nasty!"

"What is it?"

Behind me a mini-crowd has formed near one of the tables. Someone's on the ground, but I can only see the bottoms of his sneakers.

"He's been alienated," a Goth chick says, pointing. I step closer and can see it's Shaggy from trig. A steaming mass of something bubbles up from the middle of Marilyn Manson's face on his T-shirt.

"It came out of nowhere," Shaggy says, his tone half horror, half awe. "Then, like, *wham*—it hit me." He scowls. "I just got this shirt on eBay! It's a classic! Twenty-eight bucks! This giant bird turd or whatever it is better not stain."

Flynn leans down and sniffs. "It smells like . . . baked apple."

Shaggy sits up, curious. He swipes at the ooze, sniffs it, licks his finger. The other kids yell, "Ewwwww!"

"It *is* apple!" Shaggy announces. He tilts his gaze up. "Who the hell is tossing cooked fruit from the sky?"

"Maybe it's, like, a promotion thing for a new dessert," one of the Hello Kitty girls suggests. Now everybody's looking up, waiting for some blimp to sail by advertising Birds Eye's new microwaveable turnovers.

I'm not looking up, though. My eyes stay locked on the apple. It came out of nowhere. There was nothing and now there's something. . . .

That's not true, though. There was never *nothing*. There were always protons and neutrons and electrons. They've been rearranged, that's all. It wasn't what I pictured, but hey, it was my first try.

The crowd breaks up. Flynn tosses Shaggy a stack of napkins. Lunchers finish their meals and go back inside. I'm frozen in place as time moves past, until it's only me and the empty tables and my memory of Shaggy lying there, apple spattered.

Apple + sugar + flour + butter . . .

I clutch the pencil a little lighter in my hand, and I feel a small smile spread across my face.

I did it.

★ ★ ★

I'm so hyped up from my success that I stop by Ms. Lammers's class on my way to sixth period and ask her if I can do an extra-credit report on the Ch'ing Dynasty or scrub the dry-erase boards after school or walk her dogs for two weeks—if she'll give me my cell back. And then, like magic, she gives it to me for nothing! (Except for the promise that she will never see it again in class, a wish I grant immediately.) My confidence isn't quite high enough yet to brave a plea to Madame K for my sketchbook, so I leave that miracle for later.

In seventh period, I text Posh from the library computers to tell her what happened. There are so many exclamation points and all-caps in her response that I glance around a couple of times, worried that her digital yelling is audible. We need to continue this conversion verbally, but not here, obviously.

After Ms. Insardi, the librarian, gives me a hall pass "for the bathroom," I slip out the nearest exit, which opens onto the faculty parking lot. Too out-in-the-open. What if some teacher leaves early?

Around the corner is the lunch patio, now empty and apple-free. I'm right next to the window of the cafeteria kitchen, where the cooking class is learning how to make kiwi-mocha mousse or eucalyptus pesto or whatever. There's a bench along the wall, and I sit down, out of view, and dial Posh. She starts talking before she even knows it's me. "You need to keep a detailed record of everything that happens from now on."

"I'm not going to have time to do that, Posh," I whisper. "I'm going to be too busy granting wishes."

"This is IMPORTANT research, Delaney." She's so excited, she's even talking in capital letters now. "Nobel Prize–worthy. It's your responsibility to science."

"I only imploded an apple. It's not like I split an atom or accelerated a particle or something."

"But, Delaney. You sort of *did*."

"Did I?" Maybe I did. I gaze out over the patio and the scene plays again in my mind. I can see myself holding the pencil, and Shaggy Boy falling, and the other kids calling out their amazement—and *I'm* amazed all over again too.

The memory fades a little, except for the image of me, which seems to grow sharper and brighter. I feel myself, my real, right-now self, filling with energy.

More than one chemical reaction took place out on that patio during lunch.

Delaney Collins → f.g.

chapter six

"It was probably just a coincidence." Hank swats away my news like it's some annoying insect he can't be bothered with. He doesn't even look at me; he's too busy squinting down at the veggie stir-fry recipe in *Easy Dinners for Two*. He's added a big cup of "wise capable parent" to his usual "Dr. Hank" hyperanalyzing bossiness. It makes him doubly annoying, since both alter egos are so bogus. He's obviously never cooked a meal in his life, and his lecturing sounds like he's snatched a bunch of random phrases out of his books and then scrambled them together. "You wanted something to happen and so you sought evidence to support that desire, which you then extrapolated to conclude that you had achieved the goal." *Voilà,* the psychobabble omelet. If his writing is as convoluted as his speech then people must buy so many of his books because they keep hoping he'll finally write one that they can understand.

"Right," I say from my seat across the counter. "Because baked apples appear out of nowhere and torpedo random metalheads every day. It's as common as fathers calling their daughters liars."

Hank concentrates on slicing an onion into identical quarter-moons and doesn't answer. I know he has no comeback. After a night spent convincing me that the illogical is logical, he can't just rewind or else *he's* the liar. It's too late anyway, because I believe now, and that can't be erased.

"Are you *sure* it was apple?" He carefully scoops chopped ginger into a tablespoon, then levels it off with the back of a knife. He tips the ginger into one of the little bowls he's got lined up, one for each ingredient in the stir-fry he's making, like he's prepping for a cooking show.

"What does *that* matter? If it was peach, does that mean it was leprechauns who caused it and not a fairy godmother? Does blueberry mean wood sprites?"

Hank is now looking at his watch, timing the heating of the pan to the exact second. I can't take it anymore, and I march over and hip-check him aside as he's fiddling with the flame.

"Delaney."

"This is *not* how you make a stir-fry." Mom didn't cook much either, but when she did, there was no measuring spices, no whipping out the ruler to make sure the green pepper slices were exactly one-quarter inch each. She'd just grab a bunch of whatever from the fridge and the pantry, toss it all together, and make something amazing. *That* was magic.

A missing-Mom pang hits me, right in the chest, so I snap back to the two important tasks at hand: (1) stir-fry, (2) apple pie. "You overanalyze *everything*." I pour oil into the pan and empty the bowls on top of it, sending up a smoky sizzle. Hank hovers nervously behind me and I can tell he wants to snatch the spatula out of my hand. I'd like to see him try.

"You shouldn't have thrown everything in at the same time, Delaney."

"Who says?"

"It's right here in the recipe." Hank taps the page and then keeps tapping like he can will me to read it. "There are steps. See? They're numbered. There's a precise way you're supposed to do it."

"Oh well," I say with a sad sigh. "Too late." I stir the vegetables. They snap and hiss in a cloud of ginger-scented steam.

Hank folds his arms. "Listen, Delaney, I'm not saying I don't believe you about the apple—"

"Yes, you *are*."

"There was only this one incident, correct?"

"One so *far*." The rice boils over, and he has to stop arguing with me to deal with it.

He doesn't say anything more while I finish cooking, but he starts right up again as soon as we sit down to eat.

"Okay, say this *was* proof that you've inherited—"

"It *was*."

"It wasn't something you achieved easily, however, or successfully."

We're sitting at the table opposite each other, the long way. It's uncomfortable and weird. You can tell he never eats in here. Mom and I always ate dinner on the couch in front of the TV. Most of the time the TV wasn't even on. We'd play music and talk, or sometimes not talk and just be.

No chance of "just being" during this meal. Not with the Master Pontificator holding forth over the meal and spouting nonstop negativity. "Most likely it was an isolated incident. You might have some stunted, recessive version of the gene, but if the ability hasn't shown up before now, your experience today was probably a fluke." He scoops up the rest of his rice, the king done with his proclamation, all smug and superior. He loved the stir-fry, obviously, since he's practically licking the plate, but will he admit it? No. He's not going to admit anything that gives me a little more power.

"You're wrong. Let's go out somewhere. Back to that mall. I'll prove it." I'm not sure *how* I'll prove it, since I still don't know what I'm doing, but I know the power's not latent or dormant or suppressed or oppressed. It's *there*.

"I don't think you understand what I'm trying to tell you."

"I understand," I tell him. "You want to be the only fairy godmother in the world. Well, too late. You're not." I pick up my half-finished stir-fry and walk out.

I carry my plate into the den and turn on the TV. The couch is too stiff to curl up on, though, and it's obvious Hank never eats in here either, with the white carpet and crystal-clean glass coffee table. The stir-fry's cold now and it's lost its taste and there's nothing on TV I want to watch.

I flick around for a bit and then settle on an old movie that takes place in some medieval forest, with knights riding into battle on armored horses. It's all dingy greens and grays, made when they liked movies to look ugly because that was more "real."

Near the end, there's a big speech about fighting the odds and overcoming obstacles. It's the usual trite Hollywood garbage about not giving up and believing in yourself, but because the actors have those smart-sounding British accents, it's hard not to be inspired. It's like the captain (or top knight or king or whoever it is) is talking to me—and it's exactly the encouragement I need.

Hank's another obstacle to overcome, that's all. Like the handsome knights in their rebellion against their troll-faced enemies, I'm not giving up.

★ ★ ★

The next morning's Saturday and Hank suggests breakfast out, trying to make up for shooting me down at dinner. I throw him off balance a little by agreeing right away. Copying the knights from the movie, I've decided on a sneak attack. I'll pretend I've surrendered—and then hit him with all I've got.

We drive to a bakery/café, which, as I predict, is yet another "made in Santa's workshop" place, with artfully arranged baskets of bread loaves behind the counter, so gorgeous they look like they belong in an art gallery. The display cases rise above my head, filled with shelves of glistening strawberry tarts, pinwheels of pistachio biscotti, gigantic muffins, tiny chocolate cream puffs and a dizzying multitude of cookies, croissants and scones, all shimmering in a glowing amber light, like the reflection of treasure-chest gold on a pirate's face.

There's a blackboard with all the breakfast items listed in pink and green and orange and yellow, with chalk illustrations up and down the sides. It's a little too flowers-and-bunnies for me, but I admire the effort.

The place is crowded, even though it's only nine in the morning, and while we wait in line to order, I scope the crowd for a possible wish. I've brought my charcoal pencil with me, since it brought me luck before. It probably looks a little weird to be holding a pencil in a café, but whatever.

I've already tried a couple of times. When we were parking, I noticed the lady behind us scrounging around in her purse for money for the meter. I willed her a quarter but it must not have worked, since she ended up asking Hank if he had change for a dollar. Then, as we were going in, a little girl at one of the outside tables was whining to her mother that she wanted sprinkles on her waffles. I waved the pencil at her plate, but no sprinkles appeared, not even tiny imploded ones.

Those were just warm-ups, though. I'm ready now. When I see one of the café workers behind the counter try to grab a poppy seed loaf that's an inch out of reach, I casually raise the pencil and point it his way.

Nothing happens.

I'm not feeling it. Not like yesterday. I can't even seem to remember what the feeling was. Somehow I knew exactly what to do—but now I don't know anything. Maybe Hank's right, and it was only a coincidence. Maybe one of Shaggy's friends pelted him with a hot apple pie from a gourmet vending machine in the cafeteria. Maybe something did fall out of the sky. Maybe it didn't really happen at all. . . .

"I'll have the pecan pancakes and a supersized orange juice," I tell Hank. "I'm going to go look for a table outside." I need air. It's too stifling in here with all these people and pastries and Hank, and it's fogging up my focus. Before Hank can stop me, a woman with big glasses and bigger hair pops up from her table nearby, having recognized him. I leave Hank trapped in the net of praise the woman has flung over him and slip out the door.

I already know there won't be any free tables. It's like the people in the land of nonstop sun have to be outside constantly or they'll shrivel. They're antivampires. Every restaurant I've seen has outdoor tables. Down the street from the café there's a guy sitting on a folding chair under an umbrella—in front of a *shoe repair shop*.

I notice Parking Meter Lady at a table by herself next to the low wall that encloses the outdoor tables. She's holding a novel in one hand and taking forked bites of her fancy herb frittata with the other. Very confident-career-woman-in-the-city. She's totally happy and relaxed. She doesn't even glance around to see if anybody's staring. That's my goal. To be left alone and make it look like it's the best place to be.

"Hey, Delaney." I turn around and see Flynn, with Shaggy and another one of his lunch-table friends. Flynn's got his ever-present necklace of oversized cameras around his neck, and Shaggy's on a skateboard, wearing yet another "antique" heavy metal T-shirt, but the shirt's too faded and stretched out to read the name of the band. The other guy is wearing a sports jacket and khakis and has a quasi-beard decorating his baby face.

"What's up?" Flynn asks me, but I guess the question is rhetorical, because he keeps talking. "This is Brendan." He gestures to Shaggy, who grunts. "And Skids." Bearded Guy holds up a palm in a mature "I'm older than I look" hello.

"Hey," I say, and continue to look around for a table, making it clear that they don't need to stop and talk to me because I couldn't care less. Flynn, being clueless, unfortunately reads the signal as encouragement.

"We're going down to the skate park on Crescent. Want to come?"

"Why?" Which means "Why on earth would I ever

even consider going with you?" but again, Flynn gets it wrong.

"I'm taking pictures of Brendan. For his fan page."

I glance over at Brendan. "You have fans?"

"It takes time to build up an online following," Brendan huffs.

"The key is to keep the content fresh," Skids says.

"What're you, his manager?" I ask.

"I write the copy." Skids retrieves a small notebook with attached mini-pen from his pocket as evidence.

"I still think we should post my photo of you from lunch yesterday," Flynn says to Brendan. "With that apple crap all over you." Flynn exchanges a snorting high five with Skids.

"'Brendan the Boardman Creamed by Fresh Produce.'" Skids makes quote marks with his fingers.

"Shut up," Brendan snaps. "And it wasn't fresh, it was cooked."

I didn't imagine it. It *did* happen.

Skids offers a new headline. "'Grilled Granny Smith Brains Boardman.'" Brendan shoves him; Skids shoves back.

"Did you see it?" Flynn asks me as his friends continue their better-suited-to-the-sandbox shoving match.

"Um, I heard about it, I think."

"I'll show you the picture." Flynn calls it up on one of his cameras and holds it out for me to see.

"Pretty funny," I say. "Let me know if you post it."

"Do it and die, Becker!" Brendan yells from the head-lock Skids has him in. Too bad. I could use the photo as Exhibit A for Hank, but there's no way I'm dragging him out here to see it. How humiliating would *that* be? Having breakfast with your super-nerd father.

"So, you want to come?"

"Sounds like a riveting day of athletic tremendous-ness and multimedia magnificence, but I'm in the middle of breakfast." I notice that Parking Meter Lady is gone and has left her half-finished frittata behind. I pull out the chair and sit.

"Alone?" Flynn, Skids and Brendan stare at me, as if this is some terrifying concept practiced only by danger-ous foreign cultures.

"It *is* done," I say, but Parking Meter Lady must've taken her relaxed cool vibe with her, because I feel weird sitting here by myself. Maybe if I had a book. I can't let on, though, so I cross my legs, fold my arms and lean back, oozing sophisticated superiority.

"Come after you're finished, then." Flynn points down the street. "The park's three blocks below Orange Grove, or you can walk in at the gate on the corner of Wisteria."

"Useful information. Thanks."

Brendan tugs on Flynn's arm. "Let's go, man. Before all the preemies show up and hog the good ramps."

Flynn waves Brendan off and turns back to me. "You could skate down." He points to my boots.

They're my biker boots, but they're not typical ones.

They aren't short and heavy with laces and lots of studs. They're sleek and knee high, and I've painted a biker on the side of each. Lady bikers with long hair blowing in the breeze below their helmets, engines revving, as if any second their bikes will zoom down off my boots in search of the nearest highway.

"I have a lot to do today. Sorry." I lean back, waiting for Flynn to get the message. I'm not uneasy anymore. I've figured it out. You *act* like you own the space—and then you *do*.

"Excuse me." I glance up to see Parking Meter Lady, clutching her refilled iced cappuccino and frowning down at me. "This is my seat." Her voice has that clipped edge, like her next line is going to be "I'm calling the police."

I stand up. My whole head's gotten hot and the heat's spreading downward. I try to pretend Flynn doesn't exist, but I catch a glimpse of him and I can tell he's struggling not to laugh. Brendan and Skids are already at the end of the block, but it doesn't matter if they didn't hear, because I know Flynn will tell them.

If I had magic skills, I'd make everybody disappear. This day cannot get any worse.

"Delaney! I found us a table inside." Hank waves from the door, and another thick helping of embarrassment is poured right on top of me. Hank looks even more "King of the Nerds" than I realized. How did I not notice he was wearing loafers—and a *tucked-in* shirt? I'm amazed I don't drop dead right there. Unfortunately, I remain cruelly alive. As I walk toward Hank, the heat in my body climbs closer to combustible with each step.

Hank's gotten us a table inside by the window and he sits down with a huge grin on his face, like he's given me some amazing toy he knows I'll love. Great. We're right where everyone outside can see me. I yank back my chair and take a seat. Flynn's still out front and he peers in the window, smile turned on all the way now. He gives me a little wave. I hate him. He calls out something to his idiot friends and then walks away, out of sight.

Now they'll spend the day mocking me and laughing their stupid snorting boy laughter. If I don't throw myself in front of a truck first, on Monday I'll be able to enjoy the whole school pointing and laughing after Skids writes up the Facebook copy describing my humiliation. Flynn better watch out in chemistry class. Anything I can find with a skull and crossbones on it is going right into his steel eco water bottle.

"What's wrong?" Hank's lost his grin.

"*You.*" I'm now absolutely positive that my head is going to explode any second.

Hank shakes his head. "So we're starting *that* again." Right. It's always about *him*.

Outside, Parking Meter Lady, who eats alone because why would anyone be her friend, holds up her empty creamer and shakes it at a waiter like a servant's bell. I pick up my knife and point it at the creamer on the table next to us, outside the window.

"Here I thought we could go out for a nice breakfast—"

The creamer shoots across the path of the waiter and hits the wall next to Parking Meter Lady—*SMASH*. Parking Meter Lady ducks and covers her face with her arms, which get splashed with cream.

Hank's mouth has dropped open in a mix of horror and disapproval. "What did you just do?" he whispers.

I use my knife to spread the melting honey butter scoop across the top of the pancakes. "She wanted more cream." I'm feeling so much better. The pressure in my head has drained out. "So I got her more cream."

Hank leans over the table toward me. "That's not . . . You can't . . ." His face is all red, as if the heat from my head has been zapped to his. I reach around him for the syrup and pour it over my pancakes in a pretty spiral while Hank struggles with his rage-induced speech impediment. "You can*not* use your magic that way."

I point my fork at him. "You said it."

"Said what?"

" 'Magic.' " Hank huffs and sputters and glares as I chew. I must admit, the food here is as yummy as it is pretty. "I guess you believe me now."

He leans back and stares at me as the truth washes over him. He's not the only f.g. anymore.

chapter seven

Hank's muteness is tragically temporary. I've barely gotten through my pancakes when he rebounds and plunges in, in full Dr. Hank "I'm the experienced grown-up f.g. and you're merely a beginner" mode. First, there's a speech about how I can't let emotion affect what I do. I have to remain neutral or it corrupts the magic energy flow or whatever. And I'm not supposed to do anything that could draw attention to me. In other words: no more flying creamers.

"We're behind-the-scenes operators, Delaney. Doing our work in secret. Exposing yourself will just unnerve people. It's hard enough convincing your client you're what you say you are. With some clients, it's better not to tell them at all."

What's the point of having superpowers if it's not about awing everybody? Although now that I think about it, pretty much every famous superhero is in the closet. They're all about masks and disguises. I don't get it. It seems like Batman would be less doom and gloom if he could tell everybody who he really was.

On the drive home, Hank finally starts explaining the powers, of which there are basically two: Object Transference (moving stuff) and Atom Manipulation (turning stuff into other stuff—so Posh was right about me splitting the atom). I'm pretty sure Hank invented these names out of his need to make it all sound less enchanting fairy tale and more boring scientific than it is. Posh'll love it.

O.T. is easier to master than A.M., so I'm supposed to practice that one first, and then work my way up to A.M., otherwise I'll end up with more apple bombs when I'm trying for apple pie. "It's like learning a sport, Delaney. You don't start out being Serena Williams. You have to learn the basics, and then train and train and practice nonstop, and if you're patient and work hard, you'll get a chance at the pros."

This means I can only do small wishes for now. With each wish granted, my powers, will get a little stronger—not only the magic powers but the empathy part too. Because, get this, you can't ask anybody what their wish is.

It's part of the keeping-it-on-the-down-low thing, I guess, plus, according to Hank: "They're likely to tell you what they *think* they want or what they *should* want or what they think *you* think they want." Aren't these the same things? "Sometimes they don't even really know what they want." So not only are we wish granters, we have to be soul readers too.

Then, once I've got the whole tuning-in-to-people's-true-desires thing mastered, I'll be ready for a client— "probably in a year or two."

A year? Or *two*? No way.

"It's like building a muscle, Delaney. You can't start with the three-hundred-pound barbells. You have to get good at lifting the little five-pound dumbbells and gradually work up to the heavier weights." He's sure got a bottomless bag of metaphors. He probably has a whole computer file full of them, to insert into his books at random spots. "That's why it's not until *after* you grant your first client's wish that you get the full powers."

What? "You said at the mall that you get the powers and the magic wand and everything once you have a client."

"Not for the first one. It's that first wish coming true that provides the spark to ignite the skills you've been developing up to that time and propels you to the next level. Like a jump start."

"How am I supposed to grant somebody's wish without the wand?"

"That's the trick."

"Whose trick? Why am I being tricked?"

"It's the way it works, Delaney. You have to start slow. If you rush it, you won't have the empathy to accurately understand the client's wish, and then the powers won't matter anyway. I had the same restrictions as you, and I know from experience that you can't get around the rules. You have to earn it."

All that life-coaching sure has made him an expert on lecturing new f.g.'s, even though I'm his first. He probably started practicing this speech the second he found out about me and then had to bottle it back up when he thought he'd never be able to use it. That's why it's all coming out in an excited gush. By the time he gets to how you can't just pick up the violin and expect to play a solo concert at Carnegie Hall, I've tuned him out.

I've already got the muscle, the f.g. equivalent of the deadly backhand. There *are* kids who can pick up the violin and play like a super-genius virtuoso. I've seen them on YouTube. I'm not spending two years of my life retrieving lost balls and filling ketchup bottles. I don't want to have to wait for the flash of light and the glowing wand. I want the big magic *now*. That means I've got to find a client.

★ ★ ★

Before school starts on Monday, I roller-boot through the halls in an attempt to cover as much wish-vibe area as possible, but nothing wafts my way. The only wish I end up granting is Principal Lee's, which is that I keep the boot wheels retracted. I don't have to do any special mind-reading or soul-searching or yearning-detecting to discover this wish, because he tells it to me out loud, and I grant it because he threatens to give me detention if I don't. Further proof that he only *pretends* to be a pal of the people.

On my way to chem class, I spot Cadie at her locker and it occurs to me that I don't have to search at all. Since my first magic success was fulfilling Cadie's apple pie wish, I'm probably destined to do her big wish too. I know from the mindless lunch-table chatter that Cadie doesn't have a boyfriend, but there must be some football star or brooding bad boy she has a crush on. All I have to do is start a conversation and then steer it in the right direction until she mentions who she's been hoping, dreaming, wishing for. The friendly banter thing is not something I've done a lot of, but how hard can it be?

I step up beside her and try to think of something to say. "Uh . . . hi." Okay, that wasn't great, but I'm not warmed up yet.

"Hi, Delaney!" No warm-up needed for Cadie Perez. Her niceness dial is already cranked to maximum.

Right. Now I need to say something nice back. A question is good. It'll get her talking. "How was your weekend?" I'm not hesitant anymore, but now I'm too loud. I sound like an overcaffeinated robot. I take it back—being bitchy is definitely easier.

"It was great! A bunch of us went to the beach on

Saturday, and on Sunday, I saw this play in Amber Hills. I'll bring you a flyer."

Great. I'm ready to transition into the main subject. As we make our way down the hall, I walk *really* slowly, to give me as much time as possible for my cross-examination. "So . . . is there anybody you like?"

"Oh, I like everybody."

"I mean *boys*."

"Sure."

"So, who?"

"What do you mean?"

I know she's a ditz, but she can't be this brain-dead. "Listen. You know those dances, where the girls have to ask the guys? Who would you ask?"

"We don't have those here. Girls can ask guys to any dance."

"But if you *did*." I'm starting to sound pissed off, which feels more natural, but it's not going to help me.

"We usually go as a group. You can come to the next one with us if you want."

I'm losing it and we're nearly to class. "Isn't there *one* guy here who's you know, less idiotic than average?"

Cadie studies me, intrigued. "Ooooh." She gets it! "There's somebody you like, isn't there?" She *doesn't* get it. "Who is it?"

"*No,* that's not—"

"Enjoy your *waffles*?" Flynn has snuck up behind us. He smiles slyly.

"They were *pancakes*. And this happens to be a private conversation, if you don't mind."

"Did you guys have breakfast together?" Cadie asks. "That's so sweet!"

"We did not do *anything* together." I glare at Flynn but he's unstoppable.

"Sorry you couldn't come to the park, Ms. Collins, but I understand. I know how you cherish your 'alone' time." He winks at me before sliding ahead of us into the classroom. Seeing me humiliated has made him dangerously bold. Dangerous for *him*.

No chance of dumping hydrochloric acid on his camera case in revenge, though, because we have a test. I try to concentrate on the questions, but I keep thinking about Cadie. I should have realized: she's Princess Charming, not Cinderella. She's already beautiful and happy. She's not the type to have a big wish, because she already has everything she wants, and if she wanted anything else, she could get it in a second, without *my* help.

Cadie was a bad choice. I need somebody desperate, somebody whose wish vibe is so strong it reeks.

★ ★ ★

Cadie's the only person here I'm on speaking terms with, though, so I'm back to casting my f.g. net wide. After French, I hear a couple of girls two lockers down from mine whisper about a fight one of them had with her boyfriend or her best friend or her ex-friend, I can't tell. I lean closer to hear better, keeping my face hidden behind my locker door, but the conversation stops. When I peek around to see if they've left, they're both still there. Staring right at me.

"Oh, hi!" I say. "I was just . . ." Once again, words fail me. The girls glare at me, waiting for me to finish the sentence. I'm waiting too. Finally, I go with: "Does either of you have an eraser I can borrow?"

Another beat of silence, then: "No." They slam their lockers, turn their backs to me and walk off, shoulder to shoulder, continuing their whispered conversation. Too bad for them. They'll have to resolve their love/friend spat on their own.

I stroll past the other lockers, ears alert for any confessions of emotional pain. I smile whenever I catch an eye, but I can feel how fake it is. Even if I couldn't feel it, I can see it, reflected in the guarded, suspicious looks I get back. This is so not fair, because *I'm* usually the one with the force field up, and it makes me want to scream: I don't even *like* any of you!

I'm so upset that I don't notice until the bell rings that I'm on the opposite side of school from world history. I pop my wheels down, risking detention. As I speed through the halls, I succeed in avoiding Principal Lee, but I fail in getting to class on time, and I miss a pop quiz, which Ms. Lammers refuses to let me make up.

Maybe it'll work better if no one can see me.

The classic eavesdropping location is the girls' room, so I hide out there before gym. After a lot of coming and going and "How does my lipstick look?" and "Can you see my freckles or do I need more foundation?" the French snobs from Madame Kessler's class come in, in the middle of a conversation about a crush one of them has on the drummer in the marching band.

"Ask him if he'll give you lessons. Tell him we're starting a girl band."

"But he's going out with Insley Burket."

"So? You're not doing anything wrong. If Mark falls in love with you instead because you two have so much in common and he and Insley have nothing, that's not your fault."

"But I hate the drums."

Success! Sort of. I have a wisher and a wish, but I can't tell which one is the crushee, and I can't see them clearly through the cracks in the stall. I shift around, trying to get a better view—and accidentally ram my elbow into the giant toilet paper holder. Why do they call it the funny bone, when it is *so* not funny?

"Ow! Damn stupid—" I catch myself, but it's a little late. I can feel the girls' stares in the silence that follows, burning into the door. I'm surprised the steel doesn't melt.

"Hello?" one of them says, and not in a friendly way.

I have no choice, so I come out. "Oh, hey," I say, like I'm really surprised to see them and had absolutely no idea anyone was in the bathroom except me.

"Were you spying on us?" one of them demands.

"What? No, why would I—"

"What did you hear?" asks the other one.

"Nothing." I should stop there, but how can I drop this opportunity when it might be my only chance? "But if there *is* something—or someone—you want, I might be able to help you."

"I knew it!" says the first one.

"Get out!" This comes from both of them, not at the same time, but repeatedly and alternately, in increasing decibels, rising from scream to shriek. "Get out! *Get out!* GET OUT!"

"All right! Forget I said anything." Like I'd want to help either of them anyway. I still don't know which of them loves Mark the drummer, but neither one of them deserves him. If I ever find out who Insley Burket is, I'm warning her she'd better start tagging along to her boyfriend's "lessons."

I drag myself off to gym, late again. At least there are no pop quizzes in yoga. In the locker room, I whip on my East Lombard sweatpants and knee-high striped yoga socks (they aren't boots, but they cover the same area, so I almost don't mind them), then rush out to the gym and immediately adopt Child's Pose, which is basically kneeling forward and plopping your head on your arms. Ms. Byrd says we can "return to Child's Pose anytime," so I do it pretty much the entire class. Usually I take a nap, but today I keep replaying my failures and worrying that I really am going to have to wait two years like Hank said. It is not a Zen-ful thought.

In sixth period, in the middle of reading us yet another "here she lies in her grave" poem, Ms. Sandor is interrupted by the class phone. After she hangs up, she announces that the principal wants to see me in his office before seventh period. By this point, I'm used to everybody in the class turning to stare unsupportively, so I barely notice it. Barely.

On the way to the office, I mentally plot my denial that I was roller-booting in the halls again, because I figure this is why he wanted to see me. But as usual, I'm wrong.

"Delaney, Delaney, Delaney." Principal Lee pulls his chair out from behind his desk, then sits down so we're practically knee to knee. "Word is you've been trying very hard to make friends." He leans forward, arms folded, brow furrowed in concern. "Maybe you've been trying a little *too* hard, though? I've heard reports that some of your overtures have been . . . excessively enthusiastic."

He must be talking about my client search. I bet the glaring girls near my locker ratted me out. They looked the type to come whining to the principal.

"Would you say your actions were *inappropriate,* even?"

"No. Who told you that?" Maybe it was the French snobs. It wasn't enough to puncture my eardrums with their shrieking. This is what I get for trying to help people. I'm done with it. "I don't know what you're talking about."

"Spying in the girls' bathroom?"

I *knew* it. "I wasn't spying—"

Principal Lee holds a palm up in a "stop" sign. "Delaney, Delaney, Delaney. I'm sure there's an element of mis-understanding involved." More than an element! There's an entire *periodic table* of misunderstanding. "You just haven't had time yet to adjust to the style here. Our young people are a little more sensitive, a little less assertive in their interpersonal relations than they are where you're from. So let's find you an easier, more low-key Allegro High way to connect. What do you think?"

Like it matters what I think. Principal Lee's already made up his mind. No more library seventh period. I have to take an elective.

"How come it's called an elective if it's mandatory?" I ask him.

He chuckles and slaps his knee. "I love your sense of humor, Delaney! It's going to help you make a lot of friends, if you can just tone it down a little."

I don't even get to *choose* the *elective*. "I've signed you up for yearbook. It's a great group of kids, very friendly. You'll be a real asset to them—they need more people." Ah, the loser elective. Not that it matters in the end. There's no advanced boot design, so any elective I was forced into would be equally purgatorial.

★ ★ ★

Yearbook's in a Latin classroom. There are posters of the Colosseum and of phrases like *"Fortes Fortuna Adi-uvat"* and *"Credo Quia Absurdum Est"* taped up all over the place. Flynn's behind a desk with a nameplate that says "Mrs. Bayshore."

"Hey," Flynn says when he sees me. "Come on in." He grins at me like I'm hesitating or something, which I *am,* but not because I feel awkward or uneasy, since why should I, but because I can't believe Flynn's actually *in charge.* He's the editor? He's only a sophomore. I must be showing my doubt on my face, because he sort of straightens up and adopts a confident-leader tone of voice, which is very un-Flynn. "We're glad you're here, Delaney. The whole staff last year was seniors, so it's just us." "Us" is the gang from Flynn's lunch table: Skids and Brendan, plus the Hello Kitty trio, whose names turn out to be Elly, Hallie and Polly (rhyming must've been a prerequisite for the friendship).

"There *was* a junior," Elly, or maybe it's Hallie, says. "Sasha Galloway. But she quit to join drama club after they offered her the lead in *Noises Off!*"

"She's really funny," Hallie/Elly explains.

"She's from England," Polly adds.

"Thanks, guys," Flynn says sincerely, as if this is actually relevant information. The girls beam back at him and you can almost see the cartoon hearts floating above their heads. I don't need f.g. powers to figure out that all three are in love with Flynn, in a movie-star-crush kind of way. I never would've picked Flynn for teen idol status.

"Anyway, we want to do something awesome and different for this year's book," he says to me. "But we don't have anybody with design experience. So you can be art director."

Excuse me? I don't think so. It's bad enough I have

to *be* here, I can't be expected to *participate* too. "I'm not qualified for that position," I tell Flynn. "Sorry." I take a seat at an empty table, where I plan on doing nothing, like Brendan and Skids (if you count playing games on their PSPs as nothing, and I do).

"Come on, Delaney. Everybody knows you're this awesome artist." Flynn points to my boots. They're my "Bad Attitude #3" ultrasuede ones. Teeth marks scratched into the ankles, red and violet slashes and zigzags painted up and down the sides. The triplets nod, wide-eyed, and even Brendan grunts in agreement, while Skids takes a thumb off his game controls to flick it up before going back to his on-screen carnage. It's a million miles away from believable that anybody in this school has noticed anything about me that they actually liked. Come on, *really?* No. No way.

"That's why I asked Mr. Rosenthal if you could join," Flynn continues. This was Flynn's idea? The unbelievableness is now officially record-breaking. I'm ready to look for the hidden camera. Still, it would take a lot more than a couple of nice comments about my boots to turn me into a yearbook slave.

"Unless you want the yearbook to look like a boot, I really don't see what I can do for you."

Flynn tells his groupies to get last year's copy. He brings it to my table and sets it down in front of me. "Just take a look at it. Tell us what you think." He's not going to let me alone until I at least pretend I semi-care, so I page through.

Yawn. The usual rows and rows of the same over-the-shoulder pose, same frozen smile, same blank eyes. Although there are slight differences—darker skin, lighter hair, glasses, no glasses, boy, girl—they all still look identical. The senior photos are a little bigger and have song quotes under them, but even most of the quotes are copies.

"You can't tell anyone apart," I say.

"That's because you don't know them," Elly/Hallie says.

"A yearbook's not for knowing. It's for remembering. Twenty years from now, when you're really old, are you going to have a clue who these people are?" I point to a random photo on the page. A guy with an overbite, in a bowl cut and glasses. "This guy. What's the most interesting thing about him?"

"Ooh," Hallie/Elly sighs. "That's Paul. He's in a band."

Brendan rolls his eyes. "All the girls are in love with him."

"Really? This guy? You would not get that from this picture." I pick another, a girl with bangs and freckles. "What about her?"

"Allison Pellucci," Flynn says. "She's nice."

"She's weird," Brendan says. "She's always feeding those cats out by the Dumpster."

"Aw," Polly says. "That's so sweet."

I shut the book. "This is what I'm talking about. This is what the photos need to show."

"How?" Elly/Hallie asks. "These are the only kind of photos we have."

"They're digital, aren't they? They can be manipulated. Like a cat-face border for this girl and a guitar in the corner for Rock Star." I sketch some images onto the page.

"Awesome," Flynn says for the thousandth time. He really needs to work on his vocabulary. "See? I knew you could do it." He smiles at me, and I admit I don't mind being appreciated for once. "Okay, let's start a list." Flynn opens his laptop. "Three or four traits for each person. Then Delaney will come up with a few images for each."

"You want *me* to do all the drawings?"

"We can help, but your ideas will be better." That's true, but *still*—he *is* trying to make me a yearbook slave.

And yet, while they compile their collection of "remember when he stole the mascot head?" and "she wears like a million rings" personality markers, the ideas start pinging around in my head, the way they do when I come up with a boot design. Images flare like little bolts of lightning. No wonder they call it a brainstorm.

It's fun, actually, not work at all. This is how it felt when I launched the apple pie missile. Easy. It *should've* been how the client search played out, but now I see what I did wrong. I agonized over it instead of going with the flow. I need to de-agonize.

The three little kittens giggle at something Flynn says, interrupting my thoughts. Oh my God. Why didn't I think of this? I've got three Cinderella clients right here, all pining for their Flynn Charming. All I need to do is pick one of them and grant her wish. I'm back on track!

I'm not sure it can be so random, though. If there had been more than one true ever-after girl for Prince Charming, the fairy godmother could've picked an ugly stepsister instead, or one of the other thousand lovelorn girls in the kingdom.

"Hi, guys!" Cadie steps into the room, brushing her glossy mane over her shoulder. She's in her cheerleading uniform, which means her legs look even longer than usual. "I wanted to ask you if we can reschedule the squad photo," she says to Flynn. "I got Ms. Freeman to let us cheer for the girls' lacrosse semifinal against Stafford." Cadie smiles at the rest of us. "Why shouldn't the girls' teams get cheered too, right?"

Brendan and Skids nod dumbly, caught in the mind-melting haze of supermodel pheromones. Hallie, Elly and Polly blush and appear on the verge of fainting from the shock of being personally addressed by school royalty. Polly even lets out a nervous squeak. Amazing.

If I *could* pick a random client, it'd be even easier if Princess Cadie Charming were the target. I could throw a wadded-up piece of paper into the hallway between classes and have a 99.9 percent chance of hitting somebody madly in love with her.

"Sure. I'll check the schedule." As usual, Flynn is the only one but me who's not gaga. He opens a file in his laptop and scrolls through it. As he does, this sense of desperate longing comes over me. It's not my longing, though. It's flowing into me, from someone else. It's like I've tapped

126

into some invisible stream of yearning and it's dragging me along in its current.

Oh my God, it's happening! I've picked up one of the triplets' wish vibes. I peer around from Elly to Hallie to Polly (or whoever to whoever to whoever—I still can't tell them apart), trying to figure out which one is the Cinderella. I circle their table, pretending to look at the lists they're making and waiting to feel a surge in the vibe, but the feeling doesn't change and now I'm wondering if it's coming from all three at once. Three clients at the same time? This can't be right.

"Can you do next Thursday?" Flynn asks Cadie. "After school?"

"That's perfect!"

I head back to my seat, and as I do, the feeling intensifies. It's not coming from the girls' table. It's coming from Mrs. Bayshore's desk, where Flynn is writing something on a scrap of paper. He hands the note to Cadie.

"Thanks!" Cadie takes the paper and smiles at Flynn. He smiles back, the same smile he gave me. Maybe not quite the same. It's shyer, dreamier. *Lovelorn*. How did I never see this before? Now it makes sense that he never paid attention to her. Because he's *too much* in love with her. I shouldn't be surprised. Why should he be any different from every other boy at the school?

Although he is different in one way. If I'm feeling his wish, it means Flynn's the One, out of all of them, who belongs with Cadie.

chapter eight

Something's wrong. This dizzy, wobbly, "I need to vomit" feeling I have doesn't fit the whole mythical magical f.g. picture. Once I figured out it was Flynn's wish, I thought the yearning would ease up a little, but instead it's gotten worse. I don't remember any fairy-tale illustrations that show the fairy godmother's face turning green. No movie or TV fairy godmother ever looked like Cinderella's wish made them want to heave. They're confident and cheerful and knowing—not nauseous.

Hank said I might get it wrong if I rushed it, and I've been operating at siren-blaring-ambulance speed up to now. I bet my f.g. antenna is totally bent out of shape and is picking up all these random signals that are being flung at me and mixing them up into a big jumble. Maybe it's not Flynn's wish I sensed—it's everybody's. The girls I spied on in the hall and the French snobs, plus the Hello Kitties, and who knows who else. That's what's making me want to stick my finger down my throat. That's got to be it.

"Nope. That's the feeling exactly." Hank wheels his cart to the olive bar and grabs a plastic container. We're in the superstore of grocery markets. It's so big, it's practically its own country. Actually, it's a continent of random real countries, scaled way down. Instead of buildings and cars, there are tamale stands and tapas stalls and sushi stations.

"You're not listening. I'm telling you, I feel like I want to barf all over these olives." Nearby customers back away with worried looks.

"Let's keep it down, Delaney. Okay?"

"No. It's driving me crazy. I want to get it out, but it's trapped there, churning around in my stomach." Hank pushes past me to add some tiny raisinlike black olives to his collection. "You need to tell me how to turn it off." Hank snaps a lid on his olives, ignoring my agony. I'd like to slap the olives out of his hand, but I'm too weak from my warped f.g. affliction.

"It's unpleasant for a reason," he says. "If it felt good, you wouldn't be driven to help. You can't 'turn it off,' or will it away, or outrun it. You could go to China and ten years from now you'd still feel it." He sets the olives in the cart and wheels toward the six-mile-long deli counter.

"But you said it would take a couple of years before I'd get a client. My empathy meter or whatever isn't developed yet. I've hardly done any small wishes." I haven't done *any* small wishes, actually, but I don't have time for *that* lecture. I get a brain flash. "Maybe I have the flu."

Hank gives me a once-over. He holds out a hand to feel my forehead like I'm three years old, and I push his arm away. "You're not sick. I agree with you, though. It's happened faster than usual, but it's always easier to tap into someone's emotional wavelength if it's a person you care about."

"I don't care about Flynn. I care that all my nerves have been twisted up into tiny corkscrews. You warn me about everything else, but you don't warn me about *this?* If I'd known being an f.g. meant feeling like you have permanent food poisoning, I would've locked myself in a closet for the rest of my life."

"You're being a little melodramatic. I know the first one is hard, but that's because the feeling's new, so it's more intense. You'll get used to it after a while. Eventually it settles down into more of a mild anxiety."

That doesn't exactly make me feel better. "I don't want to get used to it. I want it *gone.*"

Hank offers me a cracker spread with some nasty mold-speckled cheese from a sample display. Is he trying to make me feel worse? I make a retching noise and wave it away. He frowns. "There's a very simple way to solve your problem, Delaney."

"What?"

"Get Flynn his wish."

"What if I'm ethically opposed to it? I'll be perpetuating the offensive male fantasy of the nerd landing the hot babe. It'd be different if Flynn had a noble wish. Like inventing solar cars. Then I'd believe I got it right, because it'd be something I'd *want* to help him do."

"The big wishes are always about love. That's just the way people are."

"People are idiots."

"This is what you wanted, Delaney, and you got it. It's bigger than you now; it's beyond your control. You can fight it—and lose. Or you can view it as a chance to help others, starting with Flynn. Who knows, maybe you'll like it. Stranger things have happened."

It's hard to imagine that my life could get any stranger.

★ ★ ★

Posh was run-on-sentences-to-the-max ecstatic at this proof that she was right, and that I now had a chance to advance the cause of "Science: Paranormal Division" even further. "It means I can't come home yet," I pointed out, but she insisted that the speed at which everything had happened for me so far, for which she had developed this complicated quadratic equation, proved that it should only take me $7x + 23^5/b^2$ days (or something like this) to get Flynn his wish.

As usual, I only understood about $\frac{1}{4}^3$ of what Posh meant, but by the end of the conversation, she'd convinced me to embrace my destiny: a lifetime of motion sickness (even when I'm standing still), balanced out by the power not only to move mountains (okay, maybe not mountains, but big stuff) and transform plain shoes into glass slippers, but to transform my *life*. She reminded me why I started all this in the first place: because it's going to be worth it for the full powers. Once I have them, I'll be powerFULL and the bad stuff won't matter to me.

The first thing I need to do is get Flynn alone so I can explain the situation to him. I'm not sure what the standard "f.g. reveals herself" procedure is, though. Cinderella's fairy godmother appeared in a sudden *poof!*, which gave some credibility to her claims of being magic. Plus they lived in a world where supernatural stuff happened all the time, so it was no big deal if some lady popped into a kitchen out of nowhere and started turning rats into coachmen. Even if I wanted to try and prove to Flynn that I'm magic, there's also the problem of my non-wand underdeveloped semipowers, which I haven't used since the flying creamer, so who knows if they're even working.

I'm going to have to be subtle. Ease into it.

"I can help you get Cadie."

Flynn stares at me blankly. Hmm. I may not have been subtle enough.

We're in Mrs. Bayshore's room, after yearbook. Flynn is always the last to leave, because he stays to clean up. Nobody ever helps him, so he was pretty surprised when I volunteered. Surprised and confused.

Now he's just confused.

"You mean help with the cheerleading squad photo? Elly's going to be my assistant, but you can come if you want. You could give us some ideas on how to make the group photos less boring. A lot of them are already done, but we still have about half—"

"I mean *you,* and *Cadie.*" I raise my eyebrows in the international "you know what I'm *really* talking about" signal.

"What are you talking about?"

How can he not know the signal? Come *on.* "I know you like her."

"Everybody likes Cadie," Flynn says casually, the way you'd say "Everybody likes pizza." He shoves a table back in place and I can tell by the force of the shove that the casual tone is a cover. Not that I don't already know this from my f.g. radar.

"Yeah, but you *like* her." I almost say, "You think she's *awesome,*" but he might think (correctly) that I'm mocking him, which is probably not a good way to start off the client-f.g. relationship. "I can hook you two up."

Flynn bangs another table against the first. "Brendan and Skids put you up to this, didn't they? I'm totally skunk-spraying their lockers." I dart to the next table and grab the edge across from him. He takes the other side, thinking I'm going to help him, but I hold it in place, forcing him to look up at me. When our eyes meet, I'm hyperaware that we're the only ones in the room. This must be the f.g. energy Hank talked about, bouncing between us, because I get another hit of wooze.

"It's not a joke. You and Cadie are supposed to be together."

"How'd you come up with that? Read some tea leaves?" He does his stupid snorting boy laugh. I don't even crack a smile.

"I happen to be very intuitive. It's like a sixth sense . . . kind of. It's genetic."

Flynn pulls the table out of my grasp and shifts it over into place. "Sorry to break it to you, Madame Collinska, but the gene's skipped a generation, because you are *so* wrong."

"I'm not wrong."

Flynn walks back to Mrs. Bayshore's desk and shuts down his laptop. "You're new here, so I'll fill you in. Cadie Perez is the head cheerleader. Whenever there's a new 'Who's Hot' list, she's number one. Always. She's homecoming queen, prom queen and Most Popular. She's out of my league. She's not even in my universe. Cadie's the type who goes out with the *star quarterback*."

"She's not, though! She's not going out with anybody. Because the right guy hasn't asked her." I do the eyebrow-raise thing again. Maybe this time he'll get it.

"And the right guy is me?"

I nod.

"Cadie told you this?"

"No. I don't think she knows. That's why you have to ask her out."

"Oh! Okay, then. That makes sense." Flynn loads his laptop into his messenger bag. "Not."

"You have to trust me."

"Why? Why do you care?"

"I . . . it's something I feel compelled to do, that's all. Like some people feed the homeless or rescue stray animals." Flynn gives me a suspicious look and I'm guessing that my "don't mess with me or I'll flay you" attitude up to now may have wrecked my credibility as a do-gooder, or at least dented it a little (a lot).

"You need to find a different community service project, then. Maybe one that doesn't involve people. How about Boots for the Shoeless!" He snort laughs again at his non-clever bit of non-wit.

"It's not funny! I have to do this. And you're the person I have to help." I don't add that "otherwise I'll be stuck in a pre-barf state of f.g. yuckiness for the rest of my life," because he obviously doesn't care about *my* feelings or he wouldn't be giving me such a hard time.

Flynn slings the strap of his messenger bag over one

shoulder, his camera case over the other. "I'm not asking out Cadie Perez. It's not happening. *Nunca.*" He walks to the door. "Sorry."

He leaves before I can say anything. Not that I have anything to say. This is not how I thought it would go. I expected gratitude. Praise, even. I wonder if this is a boy thing, and Cinderella was more cooperative because she was a girl. Of course, to be fair to Flynn, the fairy godmother in the story *did* tell Cinderella who she was first. And Cinderella didn't exactly go along with the plan right away. The fairy godmother had to give Cinderella a total makeover and then do all that pumpkin-into-carriage stuff before Cinderella agreed to go to the ball. But Cinderella's f.g. had the wand already. Granting wishes was a snap for her.

I'm getting off track. I can't worry about the fairy tales anymore. This is *my* story: a beautiful, unattainable quasi princess; a snort-laughing, wish-blocking non-prince; and a fairy godmother without a clue.

★ ★ ★

"What am I supposed to do? Tell Flynn he has to go out with Cadie so I can earn my wand? I do that and five minutes later, Principal Lee will switch my seventh-period elective from yearbook to lockup in the psych ward."

I've taken a break from homework, solving inverse functions, to call Posh for help. I'd ask Hank, but he's out on an emergency Andrea call, and anyway, I'm not in the mood for another "inspirational" metaphor. ("It's like becoming a juvenile delinquent, Delaney. You can't launch

136

right into robbing convenience stores. You have to start small, shoplifting magazines, and then move up to vandalizing the school gym. . . .")

"Oh my God, Delaney! I just downloaded this 'professional project completion system' from brainmania-dot-com. I'm going to use it to build a TV station in the garage. How it works is you figure out what result you want and then work backward. Like a reverse flow chart."

"The result I want is to get this stupid Cadie-Flynn-together-forever job done and over with, and then go back home and move on with my life."

"That's like five steps, I think, but okay, write those down. Now go one step back from the first one you said."

This seems like a waste of time, but Posh forces me to backward-list all my "goal requirements": before Cadie and Flynn hook up, they have to go out; before they go out, Flynn has to ask Cadie out.

"And before that . . ." Posh waits for me to fill in the blank.

"He has to have a personality transplant?" This seems like too big a manipulating-atoms move—nuclear level—for even the *full* f.g. powers.

"*No.* They have to *talk.*" She's right. I hadn't thought of that. Based on what I've observed, Flynn and Cadie average maybe five words exchanged per week, and that's counting when we have a chem lab.

I feel better. Less panicked and annoyed. This is something I can do. Creating situations where Flynn and Cadie have to talk is much better suited to my prebeginner amateur "I can't play Carnegie Hall yet" f.g. skills. It's one of Hank's metaphors without the metaphor: I have to begin at the beginning, because it's the only way to end up at the end.

★ ★ ★

My first opportunity to put Operation Backward Wish Granting in motion comes the next day when I'm heading down the hall after second period. Cadie is carrying a stack of her flower-decaled color-coded folders—and Flynn is coming the other way. I duck behind a row of lockers and shift my backpack around so I can unzip it and grab a pen. I act like I'm writing a note on my hand in case anybody's looking, but I really point it toward Cadie.

I make a tiny jerking movement with the pen, and all of her folders fall, spilling papers everywhere—at the exact moment Flynn passes by. Perfect timing! Okay, so I was only going for one folder, but this is better, because it'll take longer for Flynn to help Cadie pick everything up, which means more time to bond.

But does Flynn rush to his true love's side to assist her? No, he does not. Does he compliment her on her clever use of office supplies? Nope. He just stares down at the mess like a useless gaping bystander at a car wreck—while about forty other would-be male love slaves swoop in and rescue the damsel in distress.

No problem. This was only my first try. Maybe Flynn didn't want to compete with the other members of the "I

Love Cadie" crew. Next time, I'll wait until there aren't so many people around.

In the meantime, I decide to work on sharpening my skills by trying some small wishes. At first I only manage to spot like one mini-wish per class period—a fallen eraser that I lift back up to the desk, a loose, slipping barrette that I push back into place. (Okay, so the eraser hits the guy in the head and the barrette goes up so far it makes the girl's hair balloon out like there's a tennis ball under it, but it's the thought that counts. I think.)

I don't always guess right and I know when I'm wrong because nothing happens. But over the next few days, I start to see more. And more. Once I really begin to study people, I *notice* them. They stop being a formless, interchangeable jumble of Happy Highers and come into focus, one by one. I realize that everybody has something they need, want, wish. Nobody's life is completely perfect, even if it looks that way.

I start to learn their names too. Redheaded pencil-stealing cheerleader from Brit lit is Peri. The French snobs are Hunter and Kaitlynn. I can even tell the Hello Kitty triplets apart now. Elly's a closet techno-geek whose wishes usually involve increased download speed for whatever device she's on. Hallie's a little OCD and is thrilled whenever she can dig exact change out of her backpack to pay for lunch (which, not surprisingly, tends to happen every time I'm in line behind her). Polly's the best salesperson on the yearbook staff, but she's totally absentminded and is always showing up at school missing one earring—or she *was* until I came along.

The more I guess, the better I get at it. I can figure out what people want without having to stare at them so obviously. Soon, it almost seems like I know *first* and then I see it.

I will never in eight thousand years under threat of torture or electronics deprivation (same thing) admit it aloud, but Hank was right. It *is* like lifting weights. With every wish I grant, my magic grows stronger. I don't have to try so hard. Eventually I barely have to try at all. I can move objects so fast now, it's like they've disappeared from one spot and then suddenly appeared in another. When I finally get that wand, it's going to be fully loaded.

If I can ever get Flynn to cooperate.

When my next chance for "Project Completion: Flynn" comes, I'm ready. I'm skating past the parking lot after school when I see Flynn, juggling his cameras as he retrieves his keys from one of the two thousand pockets in his army jacket. Behind him, Cadie and Mia do their giggle-chat-squeal routine on the way to Cadie's car.

I spin around on my skates and draw a purple gel pen from the holster I've glue-gunned to the outside of my left boot. I aim the gel pen in Cadie's direction, and Cadie's car keys vanish from her hand—and land in front of Flynn a quarter-second later.

Cadie leans over and inspects the gravel at her feet. A few cars away, Flynn picks up the keys, but instead of delivering them to Cadie, he glances around in confusion, as if the keys appeared out of nowhere. (They *did* appear out of nowhere, but that's beside the point.) I try using the pen to move Flynn, but it doesn't seem to work on people. This is definitely a flaw in the O.T. concept.

Finally, Mia spots Flynn and recognizes Cadie's daisy key chain. She marches her perky little cheerleader self over, snatches the keys from Flynn with a glare and then returns them to Cadie.

A few minutes later, as Cadie and Mia zoom past him, out of the lot and out of his reach, Flynn remains by his car door, still in his trance, his hand still open, clutching at nothing but lost opportunity. Pathetic.

★ ★ ★

You'd think I could get something going in Chem I. It's *chemistry*! Elements combine and there's a reaction. Unless one element is inert.

During a lab, I sit on the back counter, writing down calculations while Flynn titrates some nasty-looking amber liquid. The safety goggles make him look like a super-geeky cartoon junior scientist, which is not a plus, and Cadie's only interested in double displacement reactions. For once she seems more focused on doing the experiment than debating ankle tattoo choices with Mia or giggling over another cheerleader's latest make-out session with the school basketball star.

Mr. McElroy strolls past our table. He's got the goggles on too: an aproned Hobbit. "Ms. Collins. Please?" He waves a pipette at my boots. I drop them off the counter. He swings the glass wand around again like a baton. "You too."

I jump down, and as I do, I casually point my pencil at Mia and Cadie's side of the table. Their lab handout disappears. I feel it in my hand before I see it, and quickly stuff it behind my backpack. Displacement achieved. Now for the reaction.

Cadie reaches for the handout but her palm lands on an empty countertop. She gazes around, on the floor, under her feet, over to Mia. Mia shrugs and starts looking too.

Cadie waves at Flynn. "Hey, Flynn. Can I borrow your handout?" Flynn's so caught up in counting orange drips, he doesn't seem to hear her.

"Flynn!" I snap my fingers in front of his face. He jerks his head my way, eyes super wide in goggled cartoon irritation. I'd laugh if I weren't so annoyed myself.

"You made me lose count. Now we have to start over."

"Cadie asked you a question."

His eyes narrow to magnified slits. "Huh?"

"I need your handout for a sec?" Cadie's voice has gone a little squeaky and I can tell she's afraid she's accidentally lit some fuse that's burning fast.

I force a smile so she'll know everything is totally calm and fine. "No problem." I pick up our handout and slap it into Flynn's hand.

Cadie reaches over and takes it. "Thanks!" she says, "I'll give it right back!" But she says this to me, not Flynn.

Mission: impossible.

I pull out the stolen handout, crumple it up and throw it at Flynn's head.

"Hey!" he protests. He picks up the wad of paper, straightens it out, stares at it and then over at Cadie, who's now consulting *our* handout.

He seems about to say something to Cadie, and I will him to do it, to speak out at last, to say *anything*. Instead he shakes his head, shrugs and goes back to work.

How hard is it to start a conversation? I want to scream at him. *I mean, come on, do I have to write it out for you?*

That's when I get my idea.

★ ★ ★

"Oh hey, hi. Are you sitting with us?" Flynn holds his lunch tray and looks down at me like he's not sure if he should be happy or worried.

"Only if you have room." I glance at the other chairs—which are all empty.

"Uh, yeah—okay. Sure." Flynn slides in across from me and gazes around for his friends. They're not coming, though, not any time soon anyway. I'd texted Brendan, Skids and the feline three before lunch and told them that Flynn wanted to meet us in the yearbook room because there'd been a labor strike at the printers and we had to decide before one o'clock whether to support the strike and go all online or be capitalist pigs and find a new printer. We're studying the Australian labor movement in world history, so that's what gave me the idea. By the time

Shaggy Skateboard Man and the rest of the staffettes figure out Flynn's a no-show, my plan will have been launched.

Flynn rearranges the lettuce and tomato on his Fontina panini, while I eat my Brie and pear enchilada and keep watch. I'm actually starting to tolerate the food here. I didn't even pluck off the lavender blossoms this time.

"So . . . how'd you get started on the boot thing?"

I shift my gaze from the doors to Flynn. *Boot thing?* "How'd you get started on the *'camera thing'*?" He totally misses the sarcasm and assumes the question means I'm interested.

"When I was four, my Grandpa Bud gave me one of those little Instamatics that print out photo stickers, and I took pictures of everything. I really liked bugs. Ladybugs, centipedes, spiders. I was like the world's youngest entomological photographer. I bet you didn't know that's an actual thing."

Flynn's distracted me with his personal essay recitation and I nearly miss Cadie emerging onto the patio. Luckily, she spots me and waves. Even luckier, she's Mia-free.

". . . then I started saving my allowance so I could—"

"Follow my lead," I whisper, and wave at Cadie to join us.

Flynn glances over his shoulder to see who I'm waving to, then whips his head back around toward me so fast I almost expect it to keep going, three-sixty. *That'd* be a buggy photo op. "What are you—"

Cadie takes the chair next to me and Flynn seems to

forget the rest of the question. She holds out the note I slipped in her locker. "I think this is such a great idea," she says to Flynn.

"What is?" he asks, glancing back and forth between us.

I pull the original list from my backpack and hand it to Flynn. I'd written it up in trig and then stuffed a copy in Cadie's locker before fifth period. "Sorry," I say. "I forgot to give this back to you." I try for maximum Cadie-style cheerfulness.

Flynn gets an old-man frown on his face, the lines between his eyes squinching up as he looks at the paper. "What's this?"

"Your list of questions." I give him a look to say *Just go along with it,* but it fails to penetrate his dim boy brain.

"List of questions for what?"

"You *know.* The *questions.* For the yearbook profiles you're doing." I widen my eyes and tilt my head toward Cadie. I really could not be more obvious. Any minute Cadie is going to catch on.

I didn't tell Flynn about the list before Cadie showed up since I knew he'd try to stop me. Once the play was in motion, I figured he'd have to go along, but I hadn't factored in a certain gender's inferior mental function. "You *remember,*" I tell him as he keeps staring at me, totally vacant. "We discussed it yesterday. Pick a few random people and interview them." I tap the list.

"I have no idea what you're talking about."

Cadie glances between us and then stands up. "I'll let you guys work it out. Have a nice lunch!" She gives us a little "bye-bye" wave as she moves off to join the cheer-leader tables.

I shake my head at Flynn. "What was *that?*"

He's still frowning down at the questionnaire. "This must've been in one of the old yearbook files, because I've never—"

"Forget about that. I made it up. It was just a cover story. An easy way to get to know Cadie." I shove the paper closer to him. "I hand it right to you—and what do you do? Go totally blank screen."

Flynn shakes his head. "You're not still on *this,* are you? I told you—"

"I'm still 'on it' because you still like Cadie." I know this because my enchilada has gone from swirling and whirling in my stomach to doing backflips ever since Cadie approached our table.

I pick up the questionnaire and shake it at Flynn. "Here it is, everything you need. Questions about her likes, her dislikes, her hangouts. So you can talk to her. That's your problem, right? You don't know what to say." This is a guess, but I know I'm right, especially when all of the blood drains from his face.

"Are you, like, reading my mind?"

"Not exactly. I told you, I have these skills . . ."

Flynn stands up in sudden alarm and searches the

lunch crowd. "What did you do with Brendan and those guys?"

"I chloroformed them and locked them in the janitor's closet." Flynn's eyes and mouth pop open in horror. He actually believes me. "You have nineteen seconds before the stink bomb explodes," I say. "Here's a clue: Colonel Mustard in the drawing room with the wrench."

Flynn drops the horrified expression and replaces it with an irritated one. "You know, Delaney, this weird out-of-the-box way of . . . of *being* that you have going on. I actually think it's cool. Really. It's why I was glad you joined yearbook. But *this* . . . this is too theater-of-cruelty-New-York-performance-art bizarre."

"I'm from New Jersey."

"That's not what I mean. It's . . . Just stop it, okay? I don't want you fixing me up with *anybody*." He picks up his tray. "And I don't want you in my head."

As Flynn walks off, the churning in my stomach increases to blender speed and I think, The feeling's mutual.

★ ★ ★

I dump my lunch because there's no way I can eat any more of it and not throw it up. I find a triangle of shade near the front steps of the school and spend the last minutes of lunch period there, alone. I text Posh to tell her about my Project Completion wipeout. She's so excited about getting accepted to some spring break "Teen Genius" astronomy course at Princeton (Posh's idea of vacation: more school) that her reply is nine-tenths rambling about some quasar-counting study they were doing and one-tenth "Keep trying!!!" Helpful.

"Here you are!" I look up to see Cadie standing next to me, one hand shielding her eyes. In her other hand is a bunch of folded-up papers. "I finished it," she says, and holds the stack out to me. I take it and unfold the top sheet.

It's the questionnaire, filled out. Cadie's handwriting is exactly like I'd expect, big and loopy and neat, with happy circles dotting her "i's." "It was your idea, wasn't it? You were just trying to get Flynn to go along."

"Um, yeah. Sort of."

"Well, I think you should just *do* it." She says this in her upbeat pep rally voice, hands on hips, and I almost expect her to break out into a cheer. ("Give me a 'Q,' give me a 'U,' give me an 'E-S-T!'") "I got the whole squad to do it at lunch." I glance through the other papers, a collection of ripped-out notebook pages, with only the answers written down. "It's a good way to find out about people," she says. "Everybody has hidden depths." I kind of doubt I'd find any depth hiding in the cheerleading squad, but whatever.

"Thanks," I tell her.

After she leaves, I stuff the extras into my backpack, because Cadie's is the only one I need. I read through it. She's got some off-the-radar indie bands under her Favorite Playlist section, and she's written down like ten books she's read in the last month, only one of which you can buy at a grocery store. Unless she made this stuff up so she'd have "hidden depths," there might be more to her than I thought. Not that it matters to me either way. The important thing is that I'm back on track.

In yearbook, Flynn doles out spring-break assignments. I'm all attention as I mentally multitask, flipping through different Flynn-fooling scenarios to find the ideal one for initiating contact between him and Cadie.

". . . and Delaney." Flynn's looking right at me. How long's *that* been going on? "Okay?" he asks. Uh-oh. I shrug, and if he takes this to mean "Sure" when I really mean "I have no idea what you just said," that's his problem. I'll email Hallie or Elly or Polly later and find out what I missed.

I'm packed up and ready to go when the bell rings. "Happy Easter, Passover, spring break, whatever," I say as I dart to the door. The staffettes call good-bye.

"See you later," Flynn says. Yes, he will. Or rather, he'll see me *soon*.

I head to the bus circle, where the kids with no wheels—either human-powered or fossil-fueled—are milling around. When Flynn comes out, I skate to the front of the bus circle and wave at the first bus, which is already moving. As it hits the street, I yell, "Hey, hold up," but not too loud. Just loud enough for Flynn to hear. "I can't believe I missed the bus!" I say to the air. "I need to meet my dad at three-thirty."

"Bummer," Flynn says, but keeps walking toward his car.

I skate up behind him and slap his arm. "Hey!" I say, like I've come up with the most brilliant idea ever. "*You* have a car, don't you?"

Flynn looks at me like it's a trick question—which it is. "Uh, yeah, but—"

"That's great! Thanks so much!"

He's already unlocked the doors, so I zoom around to the passenger side and climb in fast before he can say anything else. The inside of the car is a disaster. Cameras and camera equipment are everywhere. Photos litter the floor.

Flynn opens the door and gets in. "So?"

"So, what?"

"Where're you meeting your dad?"

"I don't remember the exact address," I say, although I know exactly where we're going. "Head up Magnolia. I'll tell you when I see it."

Flynn shrugs and starts the car. As we drive out of the lot, I shift Flynn's discarded photos around with my foot. They aren't yearbook photos or Brendan the Boardman shots. Instead there are blurry portraits of park-goers and off-center pictures of graffiti-covered walls. They remind me of stuff you see in museums, they are that strange.

"Hidden depths," I murmur to myself.

"Huh?"

"Nothing."

I pick up one of the photos from under my boot. It's a crumpled, footprint-covered picture of a street fair. Off to the side, a little girl holding the strings of several balloons glances back at the camera. The background is all washed-out metallics, but the balloons are vivid oranges and reds, so bright they're nearly blinding. The little girl seems sepia-toned, but there's still some color in her, in her face and in her dress, as if the balloons were reflecting off of her.

I'm impressed, in spite of myself. I hold out the photo. "You took this, right?"

Flynn shrugs.

"You don't have a lot of respect for your work, do you?"

"That's just a copy. I was experimenting with contrast in the developing."

"And then you use the leftovers as insulation. How reuse-recycle of you." I drop the photo back on the floor.

We turn up Magnolia, which is all stores and restaurants. If the big mall is the movie-studio European village, this is the sitcom set of small-town Main Street. The sidewalks are a shiny slate gray, without one squashed piece of chewing gum or crushed cigarette butt anywhere. The shops all have cute, handmade-looking signs over their doors and cheerful, glittery displays in their windows.

I spot a red awning ahead with a steaming cup of coffee painted on it. "That's it!"

Flynn pulls up to a meter. I get out of the car, and he gives me a half-wave good-bye as I walk over to his side. "Okay, well, I guess I'll see you after—"

"Let me buy you a cup of coffee as thanks," I say, and open his door.

"I thought you had to meet your dad."

"He just texted me. He's going to be a few minutes late."

"I didn't see you reading any text messages." Flynn looks at me suspiciously, but he does turn off the ignition.

"Come on, one latte. It's the least I can do. I'll even throw in a caramel shot. Unless you're more of a mint boy." Flynn grins. I've got him. I tug on his arm again, but not that hard, because I've already made the sale.

Once we're inside the coffeehouse, I dart in front of him so I can I scope out the place first.

"What are you doing?" Flynn asks.

B-i-n-g-o. There she is, in line to order. I turn around and give Flynn my best astonished smile. "Look who's here! It's Cadie Perez. What an amazing coincidence!"

Flynn starts to back out the door. "Oh no. No . . ." I block him from leaving and hold out Cadie's questionnaire. He stares at it, confused.

"Wait, is this . . ."

"It's Cadie's answers to the yearbook questionnaire."

"There *is* no yearbook questionnaire. You made it up."

"Whatever. Who cares? Look." I tap the paper. "This coffeehouse is one of her hangouts. Here's her favorite drink. All you have to do is order this. Then say hi, and drop a line about the Yokels." I point to another item. "It's her favorite band."

Flynn's eyes widen in surprise. "Really? I love them!"

"See how much you have in common?" I shove the paper at him, forcing him to take it.

"I guess." He reads through the questionnaire. "You know, these are great questions, actually. We *should* do this for yearbook. We could take a couple of answers from each person, and use the captions for the class pho—"

"Can you stop thinking about yearbook for one *second*?"

Flynn frowns. "I'm not going to just go up to her and start talking."

"Why not?"

"She'll think I'm weird. She'll think I'm trying to hit on her."

"You *are* trying to hit on her."

"No, I'm not. I came in here because *you* invited me."

"Irrelevant." I stab the questionnaire with my finger. "She answered these questions because she *believed* they were for yearbook. Which means she believed they were for *you*. Which means she wants you to know this stuff." Flynn thinks this over. "Just do what I tell you. It'll work—trust me."

"What if it doesn't?"

"You're free to go. I'll never mention it again."

"And if I don't do it, you'll never leave me alone."

"That's right. You're finally catching on."

Flynn sort of smiles, but then gets serious again. "You *really* think me . . . and Cadie?" He studies my face like he's going to find the answer there, rather than in what I say.

"I *know* it." I make sure my expression is as sincere as I can manage, which is an effort, since *in*sincerity comes more naturally to me. "And if you asked her to do one of these 'things I like to do on weekends,' she'd say yes." I hope.

Flynn glances toward Cadie, who's finished paying. She steps aside to wait for her drink, and I give him a shove. "Go order already, before the line gets too long."

"Okay, okay. If it'll get you off my back." Flynn takes a breath and trudges off like a condemned man.

While Flynn waits to order, I grab a wooden stirrer from the condiment stand and slip behind a nearby merchandise display to keep an eye on things—and look for an opportunity to help out.

The barista calls Cadie's order and puts it on the counter. If she takes it and leaves before she sees Flynn, or before Flynn gets up the nerve to say anything, this whole trip will have been for nothing. It's a tragedy to trash a good designer drink, but sacrifices must be made in the name of love and wand acquisition.

I point the stirrer toward the cup and concentrate. It's got to be slow enough for no one to notice, but fast enough that it works before Cadie picks it up. I barely move my wrist at all, and, one micro-inch at a time, the cup slides toward the edge of the counter.

Then, at the moment Cadie reaches for the cup, it falls.

Cadie leaps back, diving out of the way as it hits the floor—*SPLAT!* Flynn stares, mouth open, more awed by the fallen latte than by being within romancing range of the love of his life. I know I'm going for the big goal here—

professional wand, world domination—but I'm really starting to enjoy the little stuff. It's sort of like performing practical jokes, but with a purpose.

The barista apologizes for putting the cup too close to the edge and tells Cadie he'll make her another one. Cadie smiles her usual infatuation-inducing smile in thanks and steps aside to wait.

Flynn finally lifts his gaze from the floor, which another coffeehouse worker is now mopping up, and Cadie catches his eye. She shrugs in mock exasperation and he forces a strained, crooked grin back. Okay, that's good. At least contact's been made.

"Next." Flynn is still staring at Cadie. "Next in line!" the cashier barks louder. The guy behind Flynn taps Flynn's shoulder, breaking the spell.

Flynn steps up to the counter. "Green tea latte, please— soy!" He practically screams this, but it's better than mumbling, because Cadie hears him.

"Hey!" she calls to him. "That's what I got!"

Flynn throws up his hands and widens his eyes in the worst acting job I have ever seen. "No way. *Really?*" It's a good thing he's got yearbook, because he'd never make it in drama club.

He pays and joins Cadie to wait for his drink. They smile awkwardly at each other. "Green tea is really good for you," he says at last.

"I know!" Cadie replies enthusiastically, like they've now bonded over this random health tip.

"Soy too," Flynn says. Cadie nods. Flynn nods back, too many times. Awkward silence descends, and Flynn's eyes get that panicked "I've lost the capability for coherent speech" look. Luckily, his f.g. is here to help.

I spot an iPod in a docking station against the wall and slip closer, without letting Cadie see me. By spinning the stirrer in the direction of the iPod wheel, I'm able to scroll through the playlist until I find a song that will work. Then I use the stirrer to flick a sugar packet at the play button and *voilà*. *Le succès*.

When the song comes on, Flynn smiles, and this time his surprised look is believable because it's real.

" 'Starless Night,' " he says to himself.

Cadie looks surprised too. "The Yokels! I love them."

"I saw them in August at Williams Stadium."

"No way!" Cadie says. "I was there!"

"Which night?" Flynn asks.

"I'm embarrassed to say." Cadie grins sheepishly.

"Why?"

"Mia and I went to all four shows."

"I would've done the same thing, if they hadn't sold out." They exchange a smile, a real one. Mission: almost accomplished. I'm stabbed with an especially sharp twinge of the f.g. seasicky ache, worse than the usual yearning, probably because Flynn is so close to the object of his wish. I remind myself that the wand is practically in my hands and I feel a little better.

The barista sets out Cadie's and Flynn's drinks and calls

their names. "Okay, well, nice to see you," Cadie says, and then it happens—Flynn starts to deflate like a punctured blow-up lawn Santa, the courage leaking out of him. Before Cadie can notice Flynn's impending self-destruction, I jerk the stirrer toward her cup, but in my rush, I forget to be careful, and instead of falling again, it flies out of her hand, across the room. Oh no . . .

I bite my lip as customers yell out and duck. A super-tanned guy in board shorts is slow on the uptake and the cup heads right for him, an f.g.-fueled surfer-seeking missile. He sees it a second before it hits him and he dives to the side, action-hero-style. The cup slams into the wall, spattering green foamy liquid all over him. It's the parking meter lady's creamer all over again. Maybe I better lay off moving liquids until I'm at full power.

The barista looks at Cadie suspiciously. "I didn't do anything, I swear!" she insists. "It was like it was alive or something." The girl who'd cleaned up the other latte glares at Cadie and stomps off to get the mop again.

Flynn holds out his drink to Cadie. "Here, take mine," he says. Cadie shakes her head and says no, but Flynn presses it on her. "Go ahead. It's my favorite drink, but as soon as I ordered it I was craving a caramel mocha frap."

"Okay. If you're sure. Thanks." Cadie takes the drink and smiles gratefully. Good save, Flynn. I'm impressed.

But my respect doesn't last, because a second later, Flynn turns back into a frog. The awkwardness redescends like a heavy curtain. *Thunk.* I can sense Flynn frantically brainstorming for something more to say. His grin grows creepily big as terror slips into his eyes.

Cadie's smile falters. "Well, I gotta get going," she says.

Flynn's grin collapses. "Oh. Right. Sure."

Cadie thanks him again for the latte and eases off to the exit. I can't think of anything more I can do, since yanking Cadie's drink out of her hands a third time would be one wasted latte too many, and I let her disappear out the door.

This is seriously frustrating. I hurry over to Flynn. "What happened? You were totally hitting it off. Yokels, green latte. It was perfect!" You can practically see the pom-poms in my hands, I'm that rah-rah. "Why didn't you ask her out?"

"Have you ever asked anybody out?"

"What's that got to do with it?"

Flynn shakes his head and pushes past me to the door. "Never mind."

I follow him out. "How hard can it be when you know in advance she'll say yes?"

"She's not into me, Delaney. She was like 'get me out of here' the whole time." Flynn climbs into his car and slams the door.

I park myself by his window. "She was not. You just panicked."

"You weren't there." Flynn starts the car.

"I was two feet away!"

He frowns down at his steering wheel. "A guy knows."

"Since when? Boy brains have been scientifically proven to be denser than concrete."

Flynn grips the wheel and turns to me. "I tried, okay? You said if I tried, you'd drop it. We're not meant to be, all right?" He glances away. "We're just . . . not. And I'm fine with it." He looks so sad when he says this, I know he's lying, especially since I'm hit with another wave of painful yearning at the same time. "I'll see you back in school after break."

As he drives away, I get that weird twinge again, but it's different. It's a mix of feelings, all jumbled and confusing. When I try to separate them out, each one is like a stab. I feel bad for Flynn. I've let him down. I've screwed up and made everything worse. I'll never get the wand now.

I'm the worst f.g. in the world.

chapter nine

Dr. Hank is staring at me with a frozen grin. If I move to the side a little, the light hits his two-dimensional face and makes it seem like he's wincing. I wonder how he'd look with a mustache. I've got my charcoal pencil with me. It's tempting. . . .

"Don't even think about it," he says.

"Too late. Come on, aren't you curious?"

"You're supposed to be helping me here, Delaney."

We're at a table in Brennan's Books' café, where we've come so Hank can meet with the manager about a book signing for his latest magnum dopus, *Shape Up Before I Slap You*. (It's really *Shape Your Goals for Success,* but I like my version better. Catchier.) The bookstore is in the center of Wonder Mall's curving street. It's three stories high, and the café looks out over the sun-happy shoppers strolling below. The manager's busy taking inventory or unloading a new shipment of *The Idiot's Guide to Idiots* or whatever, so Hank told the assistant manager that he'd sign some of his old books in the meantime. My job is to smack a big sunburst sticker on the cover that says "Autographed Copy." Snore.

I take a sip of my iced chai. "Does the book cost more if it's signed?" I ask.

"No."

"Does it make somebody buy it who wouldn't otherwise?"

"It's an added bonus. Plus, a signed book equals a sold book, because signed books are nonreturnable to the publisher."

"Ah, so it's like writer fraud. You get the money, the bookstore gets screwed."

"Only if no one buys it."

"Forgive me, O Mr. *New York Times* Bestseller. All of *your* books get sold."

"Stop being a pain, Delaney, and get to work."

I sit back down next to him and peel and stick.

Hank left me alone when I spent the first day of spring break on the couch in front of the TV with a box of sugar bears on my lap, streaming the Design Channel until two a.m. No lectures about my lack of productivity.

No bugging me to "get some fresh air" or "eat something healthy." He'd just pop his head in every hour or so and say, "I'm here. . . ." Like I didn't know that already when I could hear him typing madly in his office next door and playing the same Billy Joel CD over and over and over and over.

I knew what he meant, though—he was there if I needed to talk. But what I needed was time to veg out. I hadn't even called or texted Posh. I was tired of telling her I'd screwed up *again*. So I ate dry cereal and did some yearbook sketches and glanced at the TV whenever they mentioned shoes or boots. I fell asleep on the couch, infomercials for recycled-rice-sack handbags and nanotech mineral makeup creeping into my dreams.

I could've slept through the whole next day, but Dr. Hank, life coach to the world, doesn't let anyone slide. He set down a plate of scrambled eggs with a big bouquet of chopped fruit on the side in front of me the next morning, and then announced we were going to the mall.

The breakfast *did* perk me up, I guess, because by the time we were in the car, I was ready to talk, and I filled him in on everything that had happened with Flynn.

"Am I the f.g. from hell?" I ask him now. "Guaranteed to make you unhappy forever after?"

"It has nothing to do with you, Delaney. It's the clients who have the problem. They don't want to face the fact that they need to change *themselves* before they can change their lives."

"I thought that was what the wand is for."

"Magic is a superficial fix. It only alters the surface, and it doesn't last. People need to transform from within. It's what I wrote about in *Self-Help Starts with YOU*." Hank picks up one of the signed books and hands it to me. "Look at Andrea. As soon as a spell wears off, she does something to sabotage her romance with Aaron. She comes up with excuses for why she can't see him. Or she cancels dates at the last minute. Until Aaron decides she's not interested after all, and then we have to start all over."

I flip through the book. Lots of charts and bullet points and "Ask Yourself These Questions" lists. There are even quizzes at the end of each chapter. "This is like a textbook for class."

"Exactly! If people would do the homework, they'd be capable of getting their wish themselves. Ideally, a person shouldn't need magic at all."

"Just one of your books."

"Well . . . yes." Hank shrugs modestly.

I sigh and flip the book closed.

"Don't be discouraged, Delaney. I've had clients who rejected my help too. Once you have more experience, it'll get easier to deal with the difficult cases."

"But how do I deal with *this* one?"

"You'll have to start over, work on the client, not the wish."

"Dr. Hank!" A woman with curly brown hair and

dressed in "I'm going to an important meeting" black slacks and a mocha-colored shirt strides over to us. Hank stands up, accidentally bumping into the table. I grab my chai before it spills, but a stack of signed books tumbles to the floor.

Hank and the woman kneel to pick up the books, their apologies canceling each other's out. I don't bother to help, because they seem to be doing fine on their own. They laugh awkwardly as they nearly knock the books off the table again when they both try to set them down in the same place.

"Anyway!" Ms. Mocha says to Hank, "I'm Gina! I started here two weeks ago. I used to work at the branch up in Seaside Harbor." I consider asking her if there are any harbors that *aren't* seaside, but I'm not sure she'd hear me since her eyes are glued to Hank's, and he's nodding like this is the most fascinating piece of information he has ever heard in his life—and possibly any past lives.

"I'm thrilled that you'll be doing a signing here," Gina gushes. "Your books are among our top sellers, although I'm sure I don't have to tell *you* that."

"Thank you," Hank says. "That's nice to hear." I lean back and prop my boots up on a chair to watch the show. This is much better than the Design Channel.

"I'm a huge fan. *Get off the Wrong Road and Find the Route to Happiness* helped me so much when I went through my divorce." I wonder how much homework there was in *that* one, although Gina looks like one of those answer-every-question-in-detail types, so she probably ate it up.

Hank tells her he's glad and nods and smiles and then nods some more. I take a big noisy slurp of my chai, and he glances over at me. He blinks, like he forgot I was there. "Oh. This is my daughter, Delaney."

"Hi!" Gina chirps, a grown-up version of Cadie. I give her a cool Mia wave in return.

Hank frowns down at my boots. "Delaney, put your feet down."

"No, wait," Gina says. She steps back and studies the bottoms. They're my demon boots. Like the dragon boots, the face is carved on the sole, but there are flames up the sides instead of a body. "Those are great! I've never seen anything like them." When Hank tells her I made them, she gushes some more. I figure she's just faking for Hank, but then she surprises me. "The leather's so thin here at the top. This must've taken a lot of patience or the swivel knife would've gone right through."

"Yeah." I can't believe she noticed this. "I did actually cut too close here, see?" I show her a tiny gash at the end of one of the flames.

"I used to buy old belts at thrift stores and alter them for myself. Nothing as complicated as this, though," she says, tapping the toe of one of the boots. "You're very talented."

She tells me about a couple of new books on leather design that have come in, and I move my boots so she can sit and write the titles down. It seems like she might actually be semi-cool underneath the bookstore-manager clothes. More hidden depths.

I let Hank and Gina discuss the signing and have some one-on-one time while I wander. I was pretty annoyed at the idea of Hank's having a girlfriend when I first came here, but now I'm kind of okay with it. It'd be different if we had this intense, going-back-forever relationship, like I had with Mom. But I don't feel like I'd lose anything if there was a third person in the mix, especially if it's somebody who gets me.

I find the books Gina mentioned, and although one of them is pretty basic, the other's filled with manic crazy stuff like using nails for clasps and glued-on pieces of broken ceramics and intentional rips in the leather. I decide to let Hank buy it for me, as payment for my sticker-sticking.

As I roam up and down the aisles, I glance around at the guides to growing orchids and raising triplets, at the thick volumes on the history of paper and the beheaded royals of Great Britain. There's a book for everything, which means that somewhere there should be a book that can help me with Flynn.

In the kids' section, I find a whole set of shelves with nothing but fairy tales. Picture books and chapter books and illustrated collectors' editions. Plus a whole row of tales from China and India and every other country on the planet.

Five minutes later, I'm sitting on the floor with the little kids, and like them, I've got about twenty books open in front of me. Unlike the kids, I'm not reading for fun. I'm studying. What I learn is that everybody in the world's got their own version of Cinderella and Tom Thumb and Hansel and Gretel, but instead of fairy godmothers, there are enchanted birds, magic snakes and spell-casting trees. Still, the basic story is the same: poor, kindhearted boy or girl hero; magical intervention for good or bad; problem, trouble, setback, obstacle, repeat, repeat; all is lost; but then . . . happy ending.

It's easy to see that I'm stuck in the setback, obstacle, repeat, repeat part of the story, but there's no clue in any of the books to help me get out. The magic is way above my level and the fairy tales feel too foreign. Not because they're from other countries, but because the places and people and times seem so unreal and far away. Despite the bad stuff that happens, the fairy tales all follow a comforting formula, wraping up neatly and nicely. They're not messy and complicated like real life. They never end with the problem still unsolved.

On my way back to the café, I pass by the gift area and spot a display of leather bookmarks, with beaches and birds and a bunch of other images carved into them. I grab a handful for more inspiration. I may suck at being an f.g., but at least I still have my boots.

"Hi, Delaney!" Cadie peeks out from the other side of the revolving rack. "What a great book!" She nods to the design book I'm holding, then glances down at my boots. "Do you actually make all those boots you wear?" When I say yes, she asks me a lot of questions about how I do it, and she really seems interested, so I explain how I buy old ones at consignment shops and thrift stores and then redo them.

"You're lucky you're so creative. I wish I could do something like that."

"Yeah, well. It's the only thing I *am* good at."

She notices me staring at the cupcake cookbook cradled in her arm. "It's a birthday present," she explains. "A friend of mine loves to make them." I try to imagine Mia, or any of the cheerleaders, wearing aprons and stirring batter, but who knows? I never read any of their questionnaires—maybe one of them has baking-related hidden depths after all. "She collects dragonflies too, so I've been looking for a dragonfly bookmark or pin or something to put on the ribbon when I wrap it. I love these, but all I can find is butterflies." She spins the rack to reveal a row of wire bookmarks, like big paper clips, bent into different shapes.

"These are great. I could use these on boots. Clip them on the tops." I search to see if I can find a demon face or a skull but it's all flowers and butterflies, like Cadie said. I take a few of the roses, because I can always paint stems down the sides of the boots, with thorns dripping blood.

"I'm meeting Mia and some of the other girls from

the squad over at Jill's Safari after this, to try on bathing suits," Cadie says. "You should come."

"Uh, yeah. I don't think so. Fashion advice from a posse of top-models-in-training would be wasted on me. I'm strictly 'what not to wear.' "

Cadie smiles and leans toward me, speaking in a conspiratorial whisper. "I know what you mean. They intimidate me too sometimes." I stare at her like *Is that a joke?* Cadie Perez intimidated by Mia and her fellow Cadie Perez wannabes? I don't think so.

"I'm not intimidated," I explain. "I just break out in hostility if people try to tell me what to do."

Cadie laughs. "I wish I could do that."

"Why? You want to alienate all your friends?"

"No. I just wish I could say what I think, the way you do. Do what I want. Totally be myself for once."

"How would you be any different than you are?"

Cadie gazes down with this wistful look that's a total contrast to her usual super-sunny expression. "Not be 'Cadie Perez, head cheerleader' all the time," she says. "Just be . . . Cadie." The way her head is tilted casts sad shadows under her eyes. It makes me think she *does* have a big wish, and I can't help but wonder what it is.

At least I can grant a small wish for her. I spin the rack of bookmarks. "You should look again," I tell her.

"I already went through them like fifty times. I wish my friend collected something easier to find. Dragonflies are impossible."

"Try the bottom rack. I think some were stuck together."

Cadie leans down, and as she does, I grab a highlighter from a nearby shelf and point it at one of the butterflies on the top rack near me. Its body stretches and its wings shrink. "Hey, look!" I take it off the rack and hold it out to her.

Her eyes brighten when she sees it. She's back to her hypercheerful Cadie self. "Wow! I can't believe I missed it! Thanks!" Her phone buzzes and she glances down at it. "I better go. But, hey, I know a bunch of good vintage shops. Any time you want to go, call me. We can look for boots and dragonflies, hang out. Okay?"

Cadie darts off to the cashier to pay, and as usual, her sincerity throws me. I'm beginning to think she really doesn't see the lines that divide the outcasts from the populars, the yearbook nerds from the cheerleaders.

Flynn's wrong. She's not out of his universe. She's in the same league as everybody else. She's not "Cadie Perez, head cheerleader, superstar." She's just . . . Cadie. And I think, hey, it might be fun to hang out, go boot shopping.

Whoa. *Really?* Delaney Collins and a cheerleader? *Hanging out?* I'm so dazed by this thought that it isn't until I'm walking back to the café that I realize turning the butterfly into a dragonfly was something I'd never done before, never even tried. I hadn't moved something—I'd changed it.

I'd done Atom Manipulation, and I'd done it perfectly.

170

When I get to the café, Gina is still smiling and tapping Hank on the arm every other second to emphasize a point, but Hank's turned into Mr. Freeze. He's so stiff, I'm worried I'm going to have to wheel him out on one of those dolly carts they use to haul the books around. I can't figure it out. They were totally bonding and now it's like he's ingested some paralyzing poison.

He's grim and silent all the way to the car. Halfway home, I can't keep quiet any longer. I have to know what happened.

"So . . . Gina seems *nice*," I say, and drag out the word "nice."

"Mm-hmm."

"I think she likes you."

"It's just a business relationship, Delaney."

"She was totally flirting with you."

"Don't be ridiculous."

"She gave you her cell number."

"In case I had any questions about the book signing."

"Maybe." I check Hank for signs of blushing out of the corner of my eye. The sun's bouncing too much glare off the car hood for me to tell if his cheeks are pink, but he *is* gripping the wheel pretty hard. I know he likes her, but he's gone all Flynn. What I don't know is why. He's an adult. And a famous author. And Gina likes him back. What's his problem?

"When's the last time you went on a date? Don't tell me it was Mom."

"Of course not," he says, but his grip gets tighter.

"Have you been on more than one date with anybody since Mom?"

"Yes, Delaney. Not that it's any of your business."

"How about a girlfriend, then? Have you had a real girlfriend since Mom?"

"Listen, Delaney. Adult relationships are complicated—"

"Spare me the condescending crap about how everybody under eighteen has no concept of human emotions, when adults are the ones who are all repressed and closeted and scarf down your self-help handbooks like they're fun-size Milky Ways."

"Motivational manuals," Hank says, correcting me.

"You may write them, but maybe you should read one. Do the exercises yourself." I try to remember one of his book titles to quote. *"Seize Happiness by the Throat and Choke It Until It Gives In."*

Hank smiles for a second and the grip softens. "First of all, it's *Seize Happiness and Don't Let Go.* There's no strangling involved."

"Too bad."

"And secondly, I think it's better if you stay out of my personal life."

"Hello? I'm your daughter, *Dad.* I'm in your personal life by definition."

Hank's smile gets broader and it takes me a second to realize what I said.

Dad.

It just popped out, but when I think about it, it sticks. It feels right. He's not Hank anymore, he's Dad. I'm not sure when it happened, but it doesn't feel sudden. It feels like it's been coming for a while. He's been transformed from within—or is it transformed from with*out?* Wait— whose transformation was it?

My cell rings, cutting through my thoughts. It's Posh. I answer.

"Oh my God, Delaney! It worked!"

"What worked?"

"The Project Completion System!"

"You built the TV station?"

"No, no. I finished that like four days ago. I'm talking about my parents. I used the system on them, one step at a time—and I did it! You can come back! All you have to do is ask Hank to call them and say it's okay with him."

I can go. I can go right now, before spring break's even over. I'll never have to go back to Happy High. Once again, I'll be where everything is familiar and there are actual clouds in the sky and the stores don't look like they were built five days ago and there's not one palm tree. All I'd be leaving behind is a dad I'd wanted so badly once but then didn't want at all, only to have him forced on me. And one ungranted wish. ·

"I can't go."

"I know you have to get Flynn his wish first. But after that."

"I think I might be out here for a while." I can sense Dad watching me, and listening.

Posh is quiet for a second. Then: "You're not coming back at all, are you?"

I don't know what to say. I feel like if I say no I'll be cutting the tether attaching me to my old life and go flying, out to space.

"In your last text, you know what you called Hank's house? 'Home.'"

"I did?"

"'I'm on my way home, call you later,' that's what you wrote."

Apparently I'd already grabbed the line to my new life, but my thumbs knew it before my brain did.

"Mom was right, then," Posh says. "You just had to give it time."

"Yeah."

Posh says she has to go, she has to watch *America's Top Inventors,* and I can tell she's hit her emotional limit for the day.

"So what was *that* all about, Delaney?" Dad asks after I hang up.

He knows what it was about. I can tell by his huge grin. And he knows I know he knows, so I say something to make his grin even bigger. "I did an Atom Manipulation today."

"You did? That's great! See? I told you. You have to keep working at it, and—"

"I know, I know. 'You can't just hurl yourself off a cliff right away, Delaney. You have to start small—begin by jumping out your window. And then work up to leaping off of the roof.' "

"Very funny."

I thought so, but although he's now "Dad," he's still Dr. Hank too, unfortunately, which means he can't pass up a chance to preach to me about the value of setbacks and the glories of failure, hallelujah, whatever. It makes him happy, though, so I let him rant on. And anyway, I've gotten good at tuning him out.

As he fills the car with hot air, I crack a window and call up Facebook on my phone. I know from Brendan's nonstop email blasts that he has a competition this week, and I only hope I haven't missed it. Staying means I'm not giving up on Flynn. Even if I have to transform him inside *and* out, I'm getting him his wish.

chapter ten

I've skated every computation and permutation of the walkways, and I'm growing tired of dodging the itty-bitty Rollerbladers with their decaled helmets and color-coordinated knee and elbow pads. I must've read the time wrong on Brendan's fan page, because whenever I pass by the ramps area, it's still just weenie wannabes crashing into each other and swearing. No Brendan. And no Flynn.

I've come to the park to observe Flynn in his native habitat (interacting with his fellow snort-laughing buddies and snapping photos at the speed of light). My plan is to study him, anthropologist-like, and pinpoint areas where I can use a little magic to boost his ego and snap him out of his inferiority funk.

I hope I didn't get the time wrong, because I spent all yesterday practicing my new advanced skills. Since I'll be living here now, I needed to make my bedroom *livable,* so I convinced Dad to take me yard "sailing" (that's what Mom and I called it—"sailing" from yard sale to yard sale). Posh had asked me if her parents should send me some of my stuff from storage, but those things still have emotions attached to them, with a thick glue that's going to take forever to come off—if it ever does. For now I've decided I'd rather surround myself with things that are feelings-free.

I found some old brass candlestick holders, a set of ceramic chopsticks that are perfect wands-to-be, a couple of black mugs to store them in, and a creepy-cool iron lamp with a spiderwebby shade and a green bulb that'll transform the whole room from Cinderella's castle to haunted house without me having to get rid of one doll.

I tested one of the chopsticks as we shopped. Wishes were easy to find, because everywhere you looked there were rips and tears and scratches and missing parts. I could tell from people's expressions when they lifted a scarf out of a box or inspected a wooden salad bowl that what they were hoping for was not what they'd found. Using the chopstick, I restored and replaced and mended and polished, and by the end of the afternoon I was an atom-manipulating master.

I brought the chopstick with me to the park and I've been mopping up soda spills and keeping Frisbees afloat to kill time, but it's not even a challenge anymore. I wouldn't be surprised if I didn't already *have* the wand. Maybe I'll be able to wave the chopstick and—*ta-da!*—give Flynn better clothes, a good haircut and a great car, and I'll be done.

"Going out for Chinese food?" I spin around to see Flynn coming up the path with Brendan. Flynn points to the chopstick. "They actually give those to you at the restaurants here, you know. You don't have to bring your own." Flynn smirks. Brendan snort-laughs and gives Flynn a high five.

"I found it . . . in the grass." I can hear how lame this sounds, but Flynn's thrown me off. I expected to find him mopey and depressed, but he's the complete opposite of the heartsick, heartbroken image of him I've been holding in my head since the flying-green-tea-latte incident. The yearning angst coming through my f.g. radar has calmed down a little too, or else I've gotten used to it, like Dad said I would.

I do notice Flynn's eyes flick around for a second, as if he's afraid I might have Cadie stashed behind a tree, but when he realizes I'm cheerleader-free, he relaxes again. "Hey, I hope you haven't gotten freaked out by all the emails," he says.

"What emails?"

"Elly sent out your questionnaire. She started getting answers right away and I told her to forward them to you. If you didn't get any yet, you will soon. So watch out."

"Sent the questionnaire out to who?"

178

"Everybody. I told you it was an awesome idea."

"Awesome," Brendan confirms.

"Don't worry," Flynn assures me. "I gave you credit."

"This is going to mean more work for me, isn't it?"

Flynn grins. "You can wait until after vacation to start." Brendan climbs onto his skateboard and swivels his hips like he's surfing an imaginary wave. "There's a competition today," Flynn says. "Come hang out if you want."

"I guess I can cheer on the Boardman for five minutes." Brendan gives me a salute and skates off to join the line of the other concussion seekers. I glide along beside Flynn, who's already got his camera up, scoping the park and the crowd.

When we reach the ramps, he drops his camera bag onto a bench near the competition area. "You can take notes if you want. Skids is in Hawaii, so we don't have a reporter."

"Really? You call him a *reporter*? He writes status updates. It's barely two sentences."

"It adds up. But, hey, if you'd rather, you can be my assistant."

"I am no one's assistant."

Flynn widens his eyes in mock fear and he throws up his hands in surrender. "Sorry. I meant you can be my co-camera . . . colleague . . . person."

"Thanks. But I'll just observe."

"All right, Professor Collins. Best view is from the top bench, over on the right." He points to the metal stands on the opposite side.

179

I skate over to find a seat and grab a spot in the top row. I ignore the cheering and groans and crashing of helmets and knee pads as I watch Flynn and think. What can I fix that will give him the most confidence? Should I shazam the oversized rumpled army jacket into a fitted leather one? Abracadabra the untied sneakers into motorcycle boots? Restyle the "I've never seen a comb in my life" messed-up hair?

Flynn moves through the crowd, snapping the action from every angle, joking around with the skateboarders, getting people to step aside so he can get a better shot. He glances over at me and waves, then points the camera my way. I hide my face, and when I peer out after a second, he's turned away to take a picture of someone else. I feel let down, which is stupid, and I bring my mind back to the task at hand.

I tap the chopstick against my palm . . . but I don't do anything. The more I study Flynn, the more I sense there's something else different about him, beyond the lack of lovelorn-ness. He changed somehow. He's already totally confident, totally relaxed, totally happy. He's *already* transformed from within—without me.

Brendan scores top points for his over-the-loop backflip one-eighty or whatever, and he and Flynn do this horrible manic monkey-dance to celebrate, hooting and slapping each other in the head. I don't cringe in horror at the geekiness of it, because everybody around them is cheering and laughing, and it's impossible not to join in.

Flynn sees me laugh too and he lifts his camera. I raise my hands again, but when I drop them a few seconds later, he's still facing me, and I can see him click the shutter. He lowers the camera and mouths "Gotcha," and I realize I don't have to change anything about Flynn at all. I just need to get Cadie to see Flynn the way I do—and Flynn to see Cadie the way she really is. Then there won't be anything standing in their way.

It'll be a happy ending for everybody.

★　★　★

When I show up at school after spring break, I find that it's not only Flynn—everything has changed. The wary looks are gone. As soon as I step onto the front walk, a zillion kids swarm me. I'm hailed with waves and hellos—and I mean "hail" as in painful, pelting precipitation: "Hey, Delaney." "How's it going?" "Can I add another favorite band to my answer on the questionnaire?" "When's the yearbook coming out?" "Hey, Delaney." "Hey, Delaney." "Hey."

I'm having a hard time cutting through the crowd with my usual hatchet of hostility, because the kids aren't a mass of flat background detail I can easily push aside anymore. It's not only because of the small wishes I granted before the break. In the last couple of days, I've read through most of the completed questionnaires Elly emailed to me. Knowing all their inner depths has made everybody around me three-dimensional, and I find myself answering them back. "Fine." "Sure." "I'll ask." "Hi." "Hi." "Hey."

When the bell rings I've barely made it inside, and by

the time I go to my locker and get to chem, the class is already in the middle of a lab. Mr. McElroy folds his arms and stares his dry-as-the-desert stare at me as I pass by his desk. "Sorry I'm late," I say. "The sun was in my eyes." I swear to God he smiles. It's only for a second and there are no witnesses, but I know what I saw.

"I'd advise you to invest in some sunglasses, then, Ms. Collins. You live in Southern California now. Sunglasses are not optional equipment." I flash an okay sign in response, but no smile this time. Must only happen once every ten years or so, like an eclipse.

I'm almost to the lab table when I stop, stunned by what I see. Flynn and Cadie are joking around. With *each other*.

"Life! Life! Give my creation *life*!" Flynn cries in a German accent. He uses a pipette to poke a creature he's built out of clamps and metal rulers. Cadie laughs. When the metal monster remains inert, Flynn yanks off his goggles and collapses onto the table over his folded arms in mock misery. Mia rolls her eyes, but Cadie keeps laughing.

Has it happened already? Have they connected? Flynn's definitely dropped the fear-of-Cadie awkwardness he had at the café, but there's nothing special in how Cadie's watching Flynn, no intense intensity. She's just her usual equal-opportunity friend-to-all self. It could be that the spark is there but is too faint to see yet. Luckily, I have the whole class period to fan the flame.

Mr. McElroy calls over from his desk, "Can we save the act for the talent show please, Mr. Becker?" Cadie goes back to work. Flynn lifts his head and spots me. He puts his goggles up to his eyes, like they're binoculars.

"Greetings, Late One."

"Don't give up, Dr. Frankenstein," I say, so Cadie will look up and reengage. It's tempting to make the little clamp man move, because it would be pretty amusing to see everybody's reactions, but the ensuing mass freak-out would defeat my purpose. Instead I pick up the pipette and sweep it toward the filled beaker behind Flynn. "Look! You've created a swamp beast!" The liquid fizzes and foams.

Flynn stares at the beaker a second, surprised, then yanks his goggles back on. "You're right, Brunhilda. It's aliiiiiiive." He grins over at me. "It's a miracle."

I used to watch the kids at East Lombard goofing around in class and I thought they were all idiots. I never imagined I'd be doing it. I have a good reason, of course, so it's justified. But still . . . I can almost see the appeal of doing it for no reason—except that it's fun.

"It's not a miracle, Dr. F. It's merely your brilliant calculations." I lift the beaker above my head. "Bog water combined with cheese mold releases laughing gas and forms a new species: Swampus Thingus."

"I never could have done it without you, Brunie." Flynn clinks an empty beaker against my fizzing one in a toast.

Cadie smiles at us. "You guys are so cute together!"

What is she talking about? Oh no . . . She doesn't think—

"It's time to break up this little social club, I'm afraid." Mr. McElroy has materialized at the end of our lab table, arms crossed, definitely smile-less. "That way you'll all have a better chance of passing the class instead of having to repeat it with me over summer school. As much as I would enjoy your company."

"Sorry," I say quickly. "It was my fault. I'll shut up."

"I accept your generous offer, Ms. Collins. And this will make it easier for you to keep your promise."

He moves Cadie and Mia to Liam and Aidan's table. The two soccer jocks break out in grateful grins at having Cadie brought within flirting range.

Cadie waves good-bye to us, Flynn shrugs at me, and they both act as if it's too bad but no big deal. "So, found any good chopsticks lately?" Flynn asks, and gives me a goggle-magnified wink. What is wrong with him? My f.g. radar is still picking up his wish, but I seem to be the only one of us feeling it.

After class, I hurry after Cadie so I can make it clear to her that Flynn and I are lab partners *only*. Well, lab partners *and* yearbook colleagues. And, I guess, friends. But *that's all*. Unfortunately, Jasper Riker and Bettina Wiehe cut me off the second I enter the hall.

"Hey, Delaney! Guess what? We're starting a literary journal," Bettina announces. "It's called *Calliope*."

"That's the muse of epic poetry," Jasper explains.

"We studied the muses in world lit last year," Bettina says.

"That's fascinating info," I tell them. "Good luck with that."

"It's not just poetry, though," Jasper says. "There'll be stories and photos and drawings and songs. All sorts of art stuff."

"It won't start until next year. We're going to meet over the summer and plan everything. And we want *you* to be a co-editor." Bettina points both of her index fingers at me for emphasis, so I know she definitely means *me*. The bell rings before I've even begun to reply. "We'll tell you more about it later," Bettina says, and dashes off to class.

In the few weeks since I've become an f.g., I've been late to class more times than in my entire life in New Jersey. If it keeps up, Principal Lee is going to drag me into his office for another "friendly" talk about my latest transgression.

I'm not stupid enough to try a funny excuse with Madame Kessler like I did with Mr. McElroy. *"Je suis désolée"* is all I say as I slink into the room. She smiles anyway, though. I hope her smile only comes every ten years or so too, because it's *très* scary.

★ ★ ★

Chemistry class was the only place that Cadie's and Flynn's paths naturally crossed, so now I'm forced to find unnatural (or rather, supernatural) ways to get them together, but day after day my attempts fall as flat as they did back when I first felt Flynn's wish.

In the lunch line on Thursday, I move Flynn's multigrain chips to Cadie's tray and Cadie's peach almond crisp to Flynn's, but although this confuses both of them, they're too far away from each other to see where their missing food has gone. Flynn grabs another bag of chips and gives the crisp to Brendan. Cadie keeps the chips and skips dessert.

Out on the patio, Flynn waves at me to join their table and Cadie waves at me to sit by her, and before I can come up with an object to transfer or an atom to manipulate in order to get them next to each other, Flynn's table is swarmed by people who want to put in their yearbook orders. At the same time, Peri and a bunch of the other B-Team cheerleaders crowd around me and bombard me with questions.

"Cadie says you make them."

"Can you make me a pair?"

"Can you make me five pairs?"

"How much do you charge?"

"Can we tell you what designs we want?"

I try to get a word in, get them to stop, get away, but they're obsessed.

"I have some plain boots at home you can use."

"I'll bring you in my pair tomorrow."

"Me too."

"How long will it take?"

To shut them up, I tell them to email me with their requests, but by then lunch is over and my f.g. objective remains unattained.

I try again in yearbook. "We should take more photos of the cheerleaders," I tell Flynn. "We can do it right now. They're down on the sports field, practicing."

Flynn looks at me like I told him to set the classroom on fire. "What are you talking about? The photos are done. We need to get going on the layout. We had forty-seven more orders today."

"Forty-eight!" Polly chimes in.

"More books means we have to budget more time for production. How many designs have you finished for the class pages?"

"Um . . ."

"Delaney. There's a deadline." He raises his arms, his hands like monster claws. "And it's looming." He drops the act and gets extra serious. "Go work on it now. Get Hallie and Elly to help you organize them."

I salute. "Yes, sir, General." It's great that he's being all Mr. Editor-in-Charge, but what's the point if Cadie's not seeing it?

★　★　★

When I get home from school that night, I turn up my music, throw myself down on the bed and wait for the usual depression to sink in.

But it doesn't happen.

I should be miserable because I've gotten absolutely nowhere this week. In fact, I've gone backward. Nothing has changed.

And yet . . . everything is different.

I'm not Delaney Collins, semi-orphan, social soloist, anymore. Now I'm Delaney Collins, f.g., *plus* yearbook art director, literary journal editor *and* boot-making entrepreneur. In New Jersey, I had one friend, Posh. Now I have Posh, Flynn, everybody else from yearbook and about a hundred other people who could be friends. So many things have been added to my life, I should feel crushed by all of it, but instead I feel weightless. My world's been stretched like a balloon that starts out an inch long and expands and expands until you think it's going to burst—and then gets bigger still. The strangest part is that it makes me feel like I've expanded too and am floating, up, up . . .

"Do you have a lot of homework tonight?" Dad peers in from the doorway.

Well, that yanks me right off my cloud of hokey happiness. Somehow I forgot about the two papers I have due next week, the trig test tomorrow and the stupid three-hundred-word essay on agriculture in Burgundy I have to write, *en français,* as punishment for being late to French on Monday. I'll need to remember this: whenever you want to get depressed, think about homework.

"I'm resting up," I protest. "I'll get it done. Don't worry."

"I'm not worried. I wanted to see if you'd like to go out for ice cream later. Help me celebrate."

"Celebrate what?"

"Aaron proposed to Andrea." I sit up. "Wish granted." He grins, thrilled with himself. I, however, have now totally, utterly, slammed back down to earth, thanks to this reminder that I'm a complete f.g. failure.

"I'm glad things are going well for somebody."

"Life is a long road, Delaney, and there are many

potholes and speed bumps along the way. What you need to remember is that for every—"

"Okay, okay, I'll go." I'll probably have to choke down a few helpings of "the glass is half full, even if it's mostly ice cubes" along with the ice cream, but it's better than lying here mood-swinging all night long.

★ ★ ★

Of all the Shangri-La-La Utopia places I've been since I got here, this is the Utopiest. It's on the beach, next to a hotel shaped like some Arabian Nights palace, and is surrounded by a huge lawn with dozens of white tables where you can sit and look out at the ocean. Behind the tables is a line of shops, all different, but with one theme: iced desserts. There's an ice cream counter and a stand for Italian ice. There's sorbet, gelato and organic frozen rice milk. There are slushies and frappes and milk shakes and floats, etc., etc., forever. There's also every kind of mix-in and a million different kinds of cones. There are so many choices, it could give you brain freeze before you've even ordered.

"I'll have mint chocolate chip in a cake cone," I tell Dad. He seems disappointed.

"That's it? Nothing else on it? Or in it? We're celebrating, remember."

"That's why I'm getting my *favorite,* Dad," I say as sarcastically as possible so he won't try to talk me into adding pomegranate syrup or sliced papaya on top. He ends up with nonfat, vanilla frozen yogurt. "And you think *I'm* boring."

"It's my *favorite*," he says, mocking me. My attitude is rubbing off on him. I'm not sure I like it.

We carry our desserts out to a table a few feet away from the fenced-off half-moon circling the beach side of the hotel, where the hotel guests get to watch the sunset from big wooden beach chairs and have their hot fudge sundaes delivered to them on silver trays. We eat and grant wishes for the families who stroll past us, rescuing falling ice cream scoops and stopping melting chocolate from dripping on clean shirts. Maybe it's the breeze or the whooshing waves or the disappearing sun, or maybe not, maybe all that's extra, but each wish I grant makes me want to know more about the person than that they like Rocky Road or pretzel cones. I want to know what their big wishes are, the f.g. ones. It's not about the wand anymore. Not in the same way. It seems funny now that I only wanted the power to change *my* life, when there's so much more I could do with it.

"I'm sorry I haven't brought you to the beach before," Dad says. "I'm not much of a beach person."

"Me neither," I admit. Mom loved going to the Shore, but I never saw what was so great about lying on lumpy hot sand, or covering your body in grease and then doing nothing except sweating and occasionally "cooling off" by dousing yourself in seaweed-clogged water that dries sticky and washes sand into every crevice of your body. I guess this is something else I inherited from Dad. I wonder if it's an f.g. thing. The only time there's a beach in a fairy tale is when someone's taking off across the sea for Ice Island or Majestic Mountain or wherever the three-headed ogre lives. The stories with fairy godmothers tend to take place in deep enchanted forests, far away from any coast.

If there *were* an enchanted beach, this would be it. I don't know what it says about me or my life or everything that's happened, but it's New Jersey now that's far away and dreamlike, and *this,* this fairy-tale world, actually seems normal, and real. I'm even beginning to see the appeal of the ocean, with its dark endlessness—possibility stretching out in every direction. The cool breeze is pretty great too.

The good mood is back. Is this emotional seesawing between pissed and blissed another f.g. side effect? For sanity's sake, I'd rather pick one and stick to it. But now, right now, I'm not sure whether I'd choose down . . . or up.

"Since we're celebrating and eating ice cream, it seems like there should be gifts," Dad says. "Or at least one gift." Dad picks up the laptop case he's brought with him. I hope he's not planning to read me passages from his latest "motivational manual." He unzips the case, but there's no computer inside. Instead he lifts out a large, rectangular wrapped present and hands it to me.

"What's this for?"

"It's for you."

"That's not what I meant."

"I know what you meant. Stop asking so many questions and open it."

So I do. Inside is a book. It's got a gray cover with a small square photo in the middle. A little girl playing in the sand on a beach. There's something familiar about the photo, and when I lean closer, I realize.

It's me.

Very faintly below the photo, written in thin gray script, as if the letters have been etched into the cover: *Delaney*.

I flip through the book. The pages are photocopies of the snapshots and cards and letters I found in his desk, arranged in collages. It's like a graphic novel; the pictures and letters tell a story. It's as if this girl exists *now*, instead of being some faint memory from the past. I'm not sure I want to read through all the sad little letters again, though. I'm glad it's mostly photos, because those are happy. Parties and parks and playgrounds.

"I didn't want to keep them hidden anymore," Dad says. I feel tears coming, but I squeeze my toes so hard it hurts and this stops them. Dad gently takes the book out of my hands and sets it down on our table. He turns the pages. "Look, here's when we went to the carnival out by that old cider mill." There's a scattering of photos laid out on the page he's stopped at, each tilted left or right. Me on the merry-go-round, waving. With cotton candy all over my face. Standing with Dad and a clown with yellow yarn for hair. I look like I'm about three. "Remember?" His eyes are kid-bright with the memory, but I shake my head. It was too long ago, and I've forgotten. The experience only exists in the book now. "Really?" Dad says. "But that was one of our best days. You had a great time." His kiddie-happy expression turns kiddie-sad. It makes me want to wave my spoon and refill his frozen yogurt cup, but I know it won't work, because that's not what he's wishing.

"I know I did," I assure him. "I can tell from the photos." This doesn't seem to make him any happier.

The sputtering buzz of a plane interrupts us as it passes by, over the water. A banner flaps behind it, the words barely visible in the fading purple light: "Bonita Beach Carnival! Final Week!"

"Look at that, Delaney! Can you believe it? We should go." He straightens up, kid-excited.

"We don't have to relive everything in this book. We'll do other stuff. Like this." I gesture to the ice cream eaters around us.

Dad's locked onto the idea, though, and won't let go. "I know, but it'll be fun. Come on. We can go this weekend." He winks. "Don't you think it's fate that the carnival's on right now?"

I decide not to ask Dad how an f.g. could possibly believe in fate, and instead remind him about the book signing.

Dad waves this argument away. "The signing's Sunday. We can go to the carnival on Saturday."

Like I want to be seen out on a Saturday night with my dad. "I'm a little old for the father-daughter merry-go-round thing."

Dad deflates again, the kid gone, and at the same time it hits me that this is one small wish I *can* do for him. A small wish that's really a big one, and I don't even need the wand to grant it.

"Okay. Let's go." Who cares who sees me? It's not like too many Happy Highers would be caught dead at a carnival anyway.

Dad's smile is back, and I discover that even non-magic non-client wish-granting generates the f.g. energy boost Dad told me about, or else the ice cream's given me a brain-enhancing sugar rush—or maybe it *is* fate—because I'm blasted by a major inspiration.

The answer I've been looking for all week comes out of hiding. It's practically waving to get my attention. Then another idea comes zooming up behind the first.

Mr. McElroy's lecture on the day of the apple implosion comes back to me. I know how to speed up the reactions I've been trying to make happen. By using a catalyst. But the catalyst isn't magic or the wand. It's me.

⋅ ★ ★ ★

When I linger after the end of yearbook the next day, I worry Flynn will flash back to the last time I cornered him in Mrs. Bayshore's classroom after hours and tense up or freak out, but Flynn's apparently forgotten all about it. He even seems happy I've stayed behind. "This is going to be the most awesome yearbook in the history of Allegro," he says as we stack the proofs for the pages. "And it's only my first year as editor!" He takes a bow for his imaginary fans.

"Like *you* did it all."

"Ninety percent of leadership is hiring the right people." Flynn locks up the proofs in the yearbook drawer.

I open my backpack and look for the carnival flyer I'd printed off the Internet. "Doesn't 'hiring' mean your sweatshop workers—I mean *employees*—get paid? I don't recall receiving any wages."

"Your salary is the honor of working for a genius." I roll my eyes. "But I do have a bonus for you." He takes a package out of his messenger bag, wrapped in a cut-up mailing envelope folded and crisscrossed with red and green rubber bands. What's with all the gifts? It must be yet another weird custom in the land of endless sunshine and perpetual smiles. I take the package and when I tear it open, I find my sketchbook, the one that the *mauvaise* Madame K confiscated and refused to return despite the three extra-credit essays I handed in and my (nearly) genuine apology *en français*.

"How did you get this?"

"I have Señora Kessler fourth period for Spanish. She likes me. I'm very polite, unlike *algunas personas*."

"She must be nicer *en espagnol*." I'm hit with a zing of gratitude—and something else, something like: how did he even know about the sketchbook, and why did he bother to get it back for me?

"If that's not payment enough, I could buy you some Chinese food." Flynn grins. "Feel free to bring your own chopsticks."

Wait, *what*? Is he asking me out? No, he can't be. He's the one who implied that it was so hard to ask somebody out, and this is too easy. He must be joking around. Asking me as a colleague, or rather as an unpaid vassal. Cadie is his Princess Charming, remember? I'm just the catalyst.

Right. Okay. This is good, though. It gives me an opening. "There's a carnival . . ." Suddenly the back of my throat gets glitchy and my heartbeat speeds up. What's going on? I thrust the flyer at him. "Bonita Beach," I manage to blurt out. "Tomorrow night." My face is hot and I feel rooted to the ground, as if my boots are made of industrial-strength concrete. Is *this* what it's like to ask somebody out?

But I'm *not* asking him. I mean, I *am,* in a way, but not *that* way, so this has to be something else. What if I've come down with some new strain of rat plague or swine flu or mad cow disease? If so, it's really bad timing.

"Oh yeah!" Flynn says as he reads the flyer. "I've been to this before. Sure, that'd be awesome. What time?"

Time. I look up at the time. Oh no, I've got to get out of here. "Gotta go." I dart past Flynn to the door. "I'll text you."

Outside, the always-fresh spring air clears my head, a little. I remind myself: *You're the catalyst. You're the catalyst.* Check, got it.

When I arrive at the sports field, the cheerleaders have already finished practice and are packing up their gear. I park myself against a tree and open my sketchbook. I feel a flare of a happy glow at seeing my old designs, which I'd thought were gone forever. Then I remember Flynn's pleased face and that brightens the glow even more. Ugh. Stop it. *I'm the catalyst, I'm the catalyst.*

I flip to a blank page and start drawing. When Cadie approaches, I let her pass and then I pop up like I just noticed her. "Oh, hey!" I say. She turns around. "Can I ask you something?"

Cadie waves at Mia to go ahead and walks back to me. "Sure. What's up?"

"Flynn and I are going to that carnival down at Bonita Beach tomorrow night. It's *not* a date—we're just friends. You should come."

"Cadie!" Up near the school, Mia glares down at us, her hands on her hips.

"I'll meet you at the car!" Cadie calls back to her. Mia stands there a second, a statue to Exasperation, then returns to life and tromps away toward the parking lot.

"Nobody'll know you there but us," I tell Cadie. "So you can be, you know, whoever you want. Cadie Perez, head cheerleader, or Cadie Perez, Allegro High's Most Popular . . . or just Cadie."

"I don't know, Delaney. I might have plans."

"But do those plans involve dirty straw all over the ground? Nasty food? Creepy carnies and dumb ring-toss games that cost too much and are totally rigged? If not, then your choice is clear. You *must* come with us. Otherwise you'll regret it for the rest of your life. Or at least for a couple of minutes."

Cadie smiles but I can tell she's still hesitant. "You can

bring Mia." I try not to sound like this is the last thing I want. "We could reunite the original Chem One, Table Six gang." I'm sure I can trap Mia in the Hall of Terrors somehow, so Cadie and Flynn can be alone.

"Carnivals aren't really Mia's thing."

Now I try not to sound relieved. "Then just bring yourself. See what happens."

Cadie's phone buzzes. She digs it out of her bag and reads the text. She stares at the phone a beat and then shifts her gaze out toward the sports field. She has that wistful look again, and I'm worried she doesn't want to be "just Cadie" after all.

"I'll do it." It takes me a second to realize she's agreed. "I'll go. I'll be myself. I *can* be myself with you and Flynn, can't I?" Her eyes pierce into me, intense. This is weirdly serious for her.

"Sure," I say.

She grabs my arm and squeezes. "Thank you, Delaney," she whispers, before she runs off. She's way more thrilled than I expected. Maybe I've been wrong all along. She *has* noticed Flynn. She *does* know he's her Frog Prince. She was just looking for an opening.

I should be psyched, but I've got this uneasiness in my chest. Like there's something I should've thought of but didn't. It must be the reversal of the client-wish yearning. Like detox withdrawal. It must be how you know the wish is about to be fulfilled for good.

chapter eleven

It's exactly like I told Cadie: bad food and corny rides and straw scattered all around like we're in Iowa farm country instead of two miles from the ocean. There's also the sweet, salty, sticky smell of popcorn and cotton candy that reminds me of the boardwalk at the Jersey Shore. The spinning rides cause the voices of the crowd and the music and the lights to swirl around in a way that makes me dizzy, but in a good way, like when I was little and would twirl in a circle, arms out, until I collapsed in the grass, laughing.

"Okay, Delaney. We should be set for the night." Dad waves three thick accordions of yellow tickets.

We're still at the entrance because we're waiting for

somebody—but Dad doesn't know that. I've already sent him back twice to get more tickets, and I can tell he's starting to wonder why we haven't gone in yet. He's wearing jeans and looks semi-normal for once. I told him I wouldn't leave the house if he had on his usual "I'm on the way to the golf course" khakis and tucked-in polo shirt. Although *I'm* not the reason I wanted him to look less geeky.

As soon as we got home from ice cream Shangri-La, I'd texted Gina from Dad's phone, pretending to be Dad, and invited her to come. I knew she wasn't working, because I remembered how *thrilled* she was that Dad's signing wasn't Saturday night. She'd texted back instantly to say she'd be *thrilled* to join us, but she's not here.

"What're we waiting for, Delaney? Let's go."

I'm considering a fake bout of food poisoning when my cell chirps. I hope it isn't Gina canceling. I check the screen—Cadie: "Running late. I'll find you."

"Hey," Dad scolds. "I turned *my* phone off."

"All right, all right." I try not to sigh in relief too loudly. Cadie's message is no big deal. I was expecting Cadie to show up after I'd hung out with Flynn for a while anyway. Her arrival needs to look like a coincidence, not an ambush.

"Even if a new client shows up tonight," Dad announces, "I'm going to ignore them."

"That's kind of cold, Dad. Anyway, did you forget you don't have a choice about it? If the wish hits you, you're back on duty."

"I'll get their information somehow and contact them later. You're more important, Delaney." Dad smiles proudly at this demonstration of paternal prioritizing, and I feel a stab of guilt at my deception, but I know he'll be grateful to me later.

"Okay, I'm turning my phone off too," I say slowly, "right . . . now. . . ."

Luckily, I can exhale another *thank God* breath a second later, because here comes Gina. She strolls through the entrance, waving cheerfully. She's in jeans, with a white lace top under a rust-tinted velvet jacket. She looks much better out of her bookstore wear—younger and more fun. Her ratty cross-trainers kind of ruin the picture, though. Her outfit cries out for boots.

"Am I late?" she says, glancing at Dad, who is glaring at me.

"You're right on time," I assure her. "We just got here a few minutes ago."

"Gina, how nice to see you," Dad says finally. He forces a smile and I carefully step out of his sight line so he can't fire any more accusing looks my way.

"Okay then, I guess I'll go find my friends now. We'll meet up later, all right? Great!" I dash off, past the ticket booth, and slip around behind a popcorn stand. When I peer out, Dad and Gina are where I left them, exchanging uneasy smiles. I'm sure there's some small wish I could grant for Gina that would at least get them talking, but Dad would catch on and my cover would be blown.

"I'm so sorry, Gina," Dad says. Oh, no. He's going to ruin everything. "I had no idea Delaney had planned to meet her friends here." I let out one more relieved breath and stop myself from screaming *"Yes!"* because he's *not* going to ruin it! He's not going to let on that he was tricked. He knows she'd be embarrassed and he's too nice to do that to her, even if it means he has to give in to my scheme. This is what I was counting on.

"I'm not surprised," Gina says. "When I was her age, I didn't want to hang out with the 'old folks' either. We'll just have to have fun without her." They both smile. Excellent.

"How about we start with some caramel corn? Get a good sugar buzz going." Wow. He's joking around, practically flirting—*and* suggesting they eat junk food. This is going even better than I hoped. Now that he's over the shock, he *does* want to have fun with her. I knew I was doing the right thing.

I find Flynn where he'd suggested we meet, at the mechanical fortune-teller. No surprise he's got a camera with him, but only one, a little pocket-sized type, and he's snapping nonstop. His subjects are all bizarre: a cotton candy paper cone, licked clean and dropped on the ground; a rusted wheel on a lemonade cart; a little boy in tiger face paint having a meltdown because he's too small to go on the gravity spinner. Flynn's totally caught up in what he's doing, like I am when I'm sketching. I'm actually feeling a little in awe, until he tilts the camera to photograph his own foot against the straw, and I have to laugh because, I'm sorry, that is just *too* weird.

Flynn hears me and points the camera my way. He takes a picture, then lowers the camera and walks over to me. "I might create an entire photo show devoted to pictures of you laughing at me," he says. "What do you think?"

"I think if you did that, people would laugh at you for doing it."

"Then I'll take pictures of those people. And then pictures of people laughing at *those* pictures. It'll be a whole series. I'll call it 'Meta-Mockery.'"

"I'd be happy to help out by laughing at you tonight as much as possible."

"That's very generous of you." Flynn smiles and slips the camera inside one of the pockets in his jacket, then fishes out a quarter from another pocket. He nods toward the glassed-in booth behind him, where a robot genie with a chipped painted-on mustache and a lopsided satin green turban stares out at nothing. "You want to ask the question, or should I?"

"How about 'Is it a waste of money to ask a hunk of metal for your fortune?'" I suggest.

"I don't think you've quite grasped the spirit of it, Ms. Collins, so I better ask." He puts the quarter in a tray on the side of the booth, slides in the tray, and a reddish light on the ceiling inside the booth comes on.

The genie raises his palms toward us. "O great genie," Flynn says in a deep voice, talk-singing the words like an incantation, his gaze pseudo-earnestly intense. "Will this be the best carnival adventure ever?"

The robot shifts jerkily to the left and lowers his hands. A piece of paper spits out of a gap next to the coin slot, and Flynn reads it with a frown. I snatch it out of his hand. "Unlikely," it says in faded blue letters. Flynn looks at me worriedly, like I'm going to be crushed or something.

"Whoever writes these things is brain-dead," I say. "Nobody's going to put in a second quarter if all it gives out is downer replies."

Flynn smiles, relieved. "Excellent point." He takes the fortune back. "I'm going to keep this, and after we have a fantastic night, we'll come back and demand a refund."

We head over to a row of "Try Your Luck" booths. We pass the crowded rifle range and darts-at-balloons game and stop at a pitching booth where there's no line. Flynn lifts a long snake of tickets from yet another pocket and rips off five for the vendor, a tanned guy a couple of years older than us with long blond hair and a cigarette hanging out of his mouth, who then hands Flynn six baseballs. Flynn offers a couple to me, but I insist that he take the first round.

There's a big three-dimensional target propped up at the back of the booth, made of wooden hoops nested inside of each other, with a round hole in the bottom of each circle where the ball goes in. You get the most points for landing the ball in the tiny center hoop and the least for the widest one, which encloses the rest. If you miss the hoops altogether, the ball drops onto the worn artificial-grass-covered base of the game and rolls into a trough, where it disappears.

As Flynn winds up, I casually point my blade of straw toward the hoops. One after another, the balls hit the center hoop. Flynn is amazed by his bulls-eyes. "Awesome." He grins at me. "Are you in awe, Ms. Collins? Am I great or what? Huh?" It's pretty amusing. The blond guy waves at a row of toys hanging on hooks along the side wall. Flynn turns to me, his proud smile still beaming from his face. "You choose, Delaney."

It all looks equally junky: bags of tiny plastic zoo animals, squirt guns, flimsy-looking sunglasses. "It's just going to go straight to a landfill."

Flynn looks at me with mock annoyance. "That is so you."

"You mean environmentally conscious?"

"It won't go straight into a landfill if you *keep* it."

"Fine, I'll take the dog." I point to a hideous stuffed dog with baby blue fur. Breed: cartoon mutt. Exactly what I need, now that I've purged my bedroom of its little-kid aura. At least it's not pink.

Blondie hands me the dog and gives me a wink. He'd be cute if not for the stinky cancer stick, so I shoot him my standard hostile look and he backs off.

Flynn offers to buy me a round, but I suggest we go in search of better prizes. It's not a very successful search, but Flynn is too high on his "awesome" athletic feat to care. "I can't believe it. I was always lousy at baseball. Maybe you naturally improve as you get older."

"Yeah, I bet that's it."

We end up at the beanbag toss. I don't need magic to get three "X's" in a row, one after the other. "There was a pond near where we lived in New Jersey," I explain. "My mom and I used to having skimming contests in summer." I let Flynn pick out the prize this time. He chooses a bracelet of red and yellow beads and hands it to me.

"You need to add some color to your life, Delaney Collins."

This is the type of comment that normally puts me into attack mode, but it doesn't now. Even when he dangles the bracelet in front of my face, saying, "You know you love it," I don't slap his hand away or make a nasty reply. Instead I take the bracelet and put it on, letting the elastic snap against my wrist.

"You don't think it clashes with my attitude?" I ask.

"You like to clash." It's true, I do. He's gotten to know me, and this feels good, bad and weird all at the same time. "Where to next?"

As we stroll over to the rides, we pass other couples, some holding hands. Of course, we're *not* a couple, we're just two people, walking next to each other, but still . . . it makes me wonder if this is what it's like to be on a date. I've never been on one, because I never wanted to. By the time I was in eighth grade, the boys were afraid of me and I didn't care since I knew all boys were jerks.

Except Flynn's not. Brendan and Skids may be mockably ludicrous, but they're okay too. And there are other boys at the school who, now that I've learned more about them—

"Is that Dr. Hank?" A woman nearby slaps her friend's arm and points to Dad and Gina, who are walking right toward us. I grab Flynn's jacket and drag him behind a row of recycling bins. "It's my dad," I whisper.

"Really? Your dad's Dr. Hank?" Flynn squints in Dad's direction. "He looks different in person."

"*Shhh.*"

"Doesn't he know you're here?"

"Of course. We came together."

"Then let's go say hi!" Flynn gets up, but I yank him back.

"*No.* He's on a date."

Dad chats with the posse of fans now surrounding him. He leans in toward them, looking earnest and imploring. They nod and murmur and back off.

Flynn and I stay in our spying position and watch as Dad buys Gina a cotton candy, powder blue, like my dog. "It looks like they're having a good time, don't you think?" I whisper. Dad says something to Gina and she laughs. They both break off pieces of the spun sugar to eat.

"Do you want them to?"

"Of course! I set them up."

Flynn smiles slyly. "Ah, I see you've directed your matchmaking impulses elsewhere."

"Uh-huh." It's the truth, technically. I *have* directed my matchmaking impulses elsewhere . . . in addition to their original target.

Dad and Gina laugh again and amble off. Flynn and I step out from behind the bins, the danger past. We weave our way through a pint-sized mob surrounding the face-painting station and the balloon animal man.

"What's it like, having Dr. Hank for a dad?" Flynn asks.

"Challenging. He thinks he knows everything."

"Doesn't he?"

"He didn't know *me* very well, until I moved here. I hardly ever saw him until a few weeks ago. Up to then I hated him, for most of my life anyway." It's surprisingly easy to tell Flynn this. He watches me like he's really listening, and it makes the words easier to let out. "If my mom hadn't died, I'd never have gotten to know him at all." An image of Mom comes to me, skimming a stone across our pond and doing a victory dance when she beats my record of skips. Then she's hugging me, throwing me off balance, causing us both to fall into the water as we laugh. After a second, the vision vanishes, like a light going off.

I gaze up at the sky, as if I might see Mom there, but it's just black nothingness. "Why does something bad have to happen for something good to happen?"

Flynn thinks this over. He shrugs. "Life sucks." I like this answer and I like Flynn for saying it. He hands me the stuffed dog, but instead of hugging it, I hold it with one hand and punch its cute little face with the other. Flynn laughs. "Feel better?" I shrug, then pat the dog's head in apology.

"Here's what we need to do," Flynn says, "in this order exactly: fun house mirrors, caramel apples, Ferris wheel, cotton candy."

"Whoa," I say. "Mr. Take Charge."

"Just call me T.C." Flynn takes my hand and pulls me through the crowd. His hand feels very present in mine. Like all of the energy from our bodies is moving toward it, our blood pulsing in sync.

I glance over at him, wondering if he's feeling the same thing, but he's pointing ahead to the fun house. It's a rickety-looking building with a giant clown mouth painted around the entrance. We race up to the gaping grin and duck inside.

As we stand in front of the wavy mirrors that make us look fat or tall or squiggly, Flynn asks me questions off the yearbook questionnaire. We go through favorite bands and TV shows and websites, and end at favorite snack. Flynn: cinnamon-covered cake doughnuts. Me: super-spicy hot jalapeño nachos with Tabasco.

We've answered all the questions by the time we leave the fun house and get in line for caramel apples, but it feels like we've just gotten started. Like we've peeled the orange, but there's still fruit inside that we haven't even touched. I suggest that next year we should add a few bigger questions, deeper ones, questions that everybody would answer differently.

"Like what?" Flynn asks.

"Like: where would you go right now if you could go anywhere in the world?"

"You first," he says.

"That's easy. Italy. Land of shoemakers. Boot paradise. The country's even shaped like a boot."

"I'd go some place so big and beautiful and awesome that you can't take a picture of it. Some place that you stare at it and it's like you get pulled out of yourself."

I close my eyes, imagining it.

"Like the Grand Canyon, maybe," he says.

"Or Legoland."

Flynn smirks. "Right. Plain caramel or chocolate caramel?" I give Flynn a look. "I'm not suggesting that as a yearbook question. We're up next." He gestures to the caramel lady, who's waiting for our order. I like chocolate, but a caramel apple should be the real thing and I tell Flynn this. "Right answer. I was just testing you," he says, and orders two straight up.

On the way to the Ferris wheel, I take a bite of my apple. It's salty and sour and sweet, pretty perfect. This is definitely how a date should be, if this *were* a date. Which it's not.

"I've got one," Flynn says. "If you were candy, what flavor would you be?"

"Bitter lemon," I say. Flynn smiles. "And you'd be co-conut."

"Thanks a lot."

"Would you rather have chicken pox or poison ivy?"

"Poison ivy!" we say together, and the other people in line glance around in alarm, making us crack up.

When we get to the front of the line, Flynn swallows his last bite of apple and tosses his stick into the trash. I hold on to mine, because you never know when you might need to grant a small wish. A ponytailed girl leads us to our seat and lowers the bar over our legs. The wheel rises a few feet and then stops, to load the next two people.

"Give me another one," Flynn says. "A real one this time."

I study Flynn, wondering what I could ask him about himself that I couldn't guess on my own, and decide that *that's* the question.

"What's the one thing that people don't get about you?"

Flynn stares out at the merry-go-round twirling and twinkling a few yards away and thinks. "That photos aren't just pictures to me." The wheel gets going for real and the car lifts. The sounds of the carnival blend together and fade as we climb higher and higher, floating up into the night. "To me they're more real than what you see in life," he explains. "You know how a vampire doesn't cast a reflection in a mirror? It's the opposite—a photo captures the true reflection. That's what I think, anyway." Here above the glare, the stars are visible. The light on Flynn is moonbeam blue, and it might be the shadows, but his eyelashes seem amazingly long.

"That's something people don't get about your *photos*. Not you."

"I *am* my photos," he insists.

"Deep."

"*You're* the one who wanted deep."

"I didn't mean cavernous."

What he's said makes me want to look at his photos again, though, even study them, to figure out what they reveal. "I think you should do a series called Hidden Depths."

Flynn smiles. "What about you, Delaney Collins? What's your secret hidden depth?"

Our car glides in an arc over the top of the wheel and then begins to fall. I try to come up with an answer. I can't tell him about being an f.g. But what else is there? "You take the magic photos," I say. "You tell me."

Flynn pulls out his little camera and stares at me through the viewfinder. "You're not as tough as you pretend."

So wrong. "Yes. I am."

Flynn lowers the camera and shakes his head. "Some people are all soft and fragile on the outside. You can beat them up easily and they might get really bruised, but they never break, because there's a steel core inside." We slide past the hay-strewn ground and then begin to rise again. "And other people have these hard, thick shells. Because inside it's nothing but jelly."

"Are you saying I'm jelly? You're lucky we've got a bar locking us in or *you'd* be jelly—splat on the ground."

"Come on, admit the truth to Rufus." Flynn props the blue dog up on the bar. I pinch the dog's nose and Flynn lets out a howl, then talks in a high-pitched voice, like he's the dog. "Come on, Delaney, come on, come on, admit it." I laugh and snatch the dog away. "Admit it," Flynn says softly in his own voice. We reach the top again and the wheel stops.

I hug Rufus as our car rocks gently. The distant tinkling of the rides and the murmur of voices is like a sound track, turned way down low. Considering everything that's happened in the last few weeks, it does seem that maybe, possibly, the clueless little girl I used to be is still there—that even though I wanted to get rid of her, she never actually went away.

This is not as upsetting as I expect it to be.

Quiet settles over us as we watch the people on the ground below. The silence between us isn't awkward this time. It's comfortable. Nice.

Flynn pats the dog's head, and I know he knows that no answer is my answer.

I gaze out over the carnival grounds and spot Dad and Gina, far away, in front of the mechanical genie. I should probably look for Cadie, but as soon as I think this, I don't want to look.

I don't want to find her.

It's wrong, I know. I'll never be able to help anyone

else get their big wish. I'll be robbing Flynn of his. I'll have to live with his yearning right next to me, in my face, forever. I'll never get the wand.

I don't care.

The wheel starts moving again, and as we drift down, I spot someone familiar at the edge of the crowd, wearing a frilly party dress that looks totally out of place here. It's not Cadie. But it's almost as bad.

Oh. No.

When we reach the bottom, the ponytailed girl lifts the bar and we both jump up, but for different reasons.

"Next up, cotton candy!" Flynn announces, and grins at me.

"I have to, um, go to the bathroom." I shove Rufus at him. "You get the cotton candy and I'll meet you back here." Before Flynn can answer, I race off.

It must be carnival rush hour because everywhere I turn, it's packs of middle schoolers and college students making out and slow-moving little kids with even slower-moving parents. I wade through the human swamp, pushing everyone out of my way.

Finally I spot the dress. Pinky-orange with a big belted bow in front that's come untied. Too big and falling off one shoulder. When I get closer, I can see the messy permed hair, and it feels like my heart has dropped into my stomach because it really is her.

"Andrea!" I wave and run over.

"Oh, hi, Delaney." Her smile is crooked and forced, her

mascara smeared. "I'm looking for your dad. He told me he was bringing you here tonight." Her eyes dart around in impending-psychotic-breakdown mode.

"Does he know you're here?"

Andrea's smile twitches, then dissolves, and she drops her head into her hands. "It's so awful." She looks up at me. Her eyes are red and horror-movie scary, with jagged dripping black liner rimming them. "Aaron took me out to the place we had our first date, to celebrate. I wanted to look like I did that night . . . I was so beautiful." She lets out a shuddering little sob. "And I tried. See?" She waves a shaky hand at herself. "I tried to do it on my own. I bought a dress. Put up my hair." I now notice there are bobby pins all over her head, poking out from the ends of the curls, like tiny lightning rods. "But I couldn't do it. I couldn't fake it. So I left. I left Aaron."

"You broke up with him?" I glance around, hoping that Dad and Gina are nowhere near.

"No. I *left* him. At the restaurant. I had the hostess call me a cab." She clutches her hands together, her knuckles white. "I *need* the magic," she pleads, like a crack addict in withdrawal.

I take her arm and steer her back toward the entrance. "I'll tell Dad to call you tomorrow."

"No, no, no. I have to see him." Andrea struggles to get free but I tighten my grip.

"You've got to get some sleep first. He won't be able to do anything for you now. The magic doesn't work if you're too stressed out." I have no idea if this is true, but it's no weirder than the other f.g. rules.

"Really?"

"Yeah. The bad energy sort of deflects the good. Spells will bounce right off you."

"Oh." She gives up struggling. "The cab left, though. How will I get home?"

"We can get someone in the ticket booth to call another one for you." Crisis averted.

Until I hear a voice behind me. Dad's voice: "Andrea?"

Andrea spins around, plucking herself free from my grasp. She races to Dad, arms out, and in a second she's got them wrapped around him in a sobbing hug. "I can't do it without you, Dr. Hank. I *need* you."

Gina stands a couple of steps behind Dad, her eyes unblinking, her mouth gaping open like the clown's mouth on the fun house entrance. It'd be funny if it wasn't so cataclysmic.

Dad pats Andrea a couple of times on the back and smiles queasily at Gina. "Client," he says.

"She *is*," I assure Gina.

Dad tries to peel Andrea off of him, but she's holding tight. "Some of them can be a little . . . needy," he says, and smiles again, but Gina's stunned expression has frozen onto her face. Only her eyes move, shifting from Dad to Andrea to me and back.

I grab one of Andrea's wrists, squeezing hard, and she lets go of Dad. "You're not supposed to hug your *life*

216

coach," I scold, shooting a glance at Gina to make sure she's listening.

Andrea sniffs and clings to me like she's going to collapse if I don't hold her up. "He's more than a life coach," Andrea whimpers. "He's a life *saver*. A life *savior* . . . a *love* savior." She stares with tragic adoration at Dad.

"Andrea . . ." Dad shakes his head. He's not looking at Gina anymore. This isn't good.

Andrea blinks away her mascara-drippy tears and gazes around at all of us. "I've interrupted your family outing. I'm so sorry. Everything I do is wrong." She drops her head into her hands again.

"That's okay," Gina says. She tries to sound upbeat, but her voice is tense and pulled tight, like a ponytail with a too-small hair band. "I should be going anyway. It's getting late."

"But Andrea's leaving!" I protest. *"Right now."* Andrea takes a weepy gulp at this and Dad closes his eyes like he's in pain.

"It's okay, Delaney." Gina pats my arm, then turns to Dad. "Thank you, Hank. I had a very nice time. I'll see you at the signing." She glances at Andrea. "Nice to meet you."

Andrea smiles gratefully through her inky tears. "Oh, thank you. You too."

Gina walks off. Dad doesn't seem to notice. He stares straight ahead of him, back to Mr. Freeze.

"She's very pretty," Andrea says to me, her panic attack over. "You never think of a fairy godmother having a love life." She turns to Dad. "But of course, you must have. You have a daughter."

"I'm going to drive you home, Andrea," Dad says in his professional Dr. Hank "I'm in command" voice. "We'll talk on Monday. During *office hours*." Andrea nods. Dad takes me aside. "Go back to your friends, Delaney. Give me a call when you want me to pick you up."

"Go get Gina," I urge him. "Tell her to come back. It's not that late."

He shakes his head with a sad smile. "It's *way* too late."

"You were having a good time!"

"I appreciate what you tried to do, Delaney. But you have to trust me to take care of my own life." He puts his hand on my shoulder and squeezes it, and I know there's nothing I can say to change his mind.

My mood has deflated like a popped carnival balloon, but then I think of Flynn, waiting for me with cotton candy and his goofy grin, and it pumps me back up.

I feel lighter and lighter as I hurry through the crowd, texting Cadie as I go, telling her not to come, that we had to leave early, that I'll call her. I'll make it up to her later somehow. We'll go shopping. I'll design her a special pair of boots.

I spot Flynn up ahead, his back to me, holding two cotton candy cones, the stuffed dog under his arm, and I'm lifted even higher, as if my boots have air jets on the bottom and any second they'll raise me off the ground.

Then I see who he's talking to, and I crash-land to reality with a painful thud.

Cadie.

She's standing next to a girl I don't recognize. Cadie says something to Flynn and he reaches out to touch her on the arm. Cadie beams at him, warmer and more sincere than I've ever seen, which is saying something for her. It says a lot actually, and what it says is mostly about Flynn. He *is* her prince.

I close my phone, the text unsent. I feel off-balance and woozy. The air's gotten heavy all of a sudden and the swarm of carnival smells is making me nauseous—the salty-smoky scent of the popcorn, the sickening sweet of the cotton candy and the pinching sour of the lemonade. The caramel apple stews in my stomach. I have to get out of here.

"Delaney!" Cadie's seen me. She waves and hops up onto her toes, like she's about to launch into a cheer spelling out my name. She's wearing cutoffs, a bright white T-shirt and high-tops, her hair pulled back in a loose braid. This must be her idea of "being herself." Right. Really daring. She looks like a movie star getting on an airplane—dressed down but still gorgeous.

I trudge over, my bootheels dragging through the straw. Flynn smiles at me and a wave of giddy, annoying bliss gushes out of him and knocks into me. That must be what's making me so sick. I'm not going to slap the idiot grin off his face, though, because this is what I wanted. Flynn got his wish. And I wasn't even here to see it happen. It's like Dad said, you don't need the magic. Apparently you don't even need the f.g.

Whatever. What matters now is that I get the wand, nothing else. I pick up a piece of straw but it flops limply in my hand. I don't feel powerful. I feel totally sapped. Maybe some sort of recharge needs to happen before the next client, although the thought of going through all this again exhausts me even more.

"Hi, Delaney," Cadie says when I reach them, her smile as genuinely genuine as ever. "This is Emma." The other girl says hello. She's got wildly curly red hair, multiple ear piercings and is wearing an Indian tunic with lots of spirally embroidery over brown cargo pants. She's definitely not one of Cadie's cheerleading friends. She doesn't say much, and I get the feeling she's a cousin or the daughter of a family friend who's been forced to tag along. The third wheel. Left out. I know how she feels.

"I was just going to tell Flynn, I'm having a beach party tomorrow," Cadie says. "I want you guys to come."

"I'll be there!" Flynn says. Does he have to be *so* enthusiastic? Not that I care. Anymore.

Cadie looks eagerly at me. "I can't, I'm busy tomorrow," I say. "I actually have to leave now." I know I should try to lure Emma off with me so the happy couple can bond, but I can't stand to be here any longer. "My dad's got this business-related crisis. He needs me." Cadie and Emma say they're sorry and do a pretty good job of sounding like they mean it, and even Flynn's smile fades a little.

"But I have your cotton candy," Flynn says. He holds it out to me.

"You guys can share it." As I say this, I get a mental picture of Cadie and Flynn with their hands around one cone, fingers touching, their lips getting closer with every bite. . . .

"So I'll call you?" Flynn says, unsure.

I push the image away. "That's okay." I don't look at him. I don't look at any of them. I just race off, dialing Dad as I go, ignoring Flynn's last call after me: "You forgot Rufus!"

On my way to the exit, I see a little girl with sticky orange Popsicle traces all over her face and crying. I wave the straw at her but nothing happens. I can't even summon the concentration to grant a small wish. Or the will. The girl is the one who smeared the fake-flavored frozen treat everywhere. Let her live with it. I break the straw into pieces and toss them on the ground. A few feet away, the robot fortune-teller mocks me with his blank-eyed grin.

As if he knows he was right in his prediction after all.

★ ★ ★

Dad drives up to the Styrofoam hay roll I'm sitting on at the entrance to the carnival parking lot. He unlocks the door and I get in.

"That wasn't very long. I hadn't even gotten home yet."

"Everybody was leaving."

"You did have friends there, right?" he asks. "You weren't just off by yourself?"

"Why would I lie about that? I *have* friends." I'd started to think I did, anyway. Now I'm not so sure. "It was a bunch of people from school."

"And they all decided to go home at once."

"There's not much to do here, in case you didn't notice. We'd hit all the rides, played the games, had a candy apple. What's left?"

"Did something happen, Delaney? Something you're not telling me?"

"Nope. Nothing happened." Nothing at all. To stop any further interrogation, I direct the conversation back to him. "How's Andrea?"

"Fine." Now *he's* the one who doesn't want to talk, which is more than okay with me, because I'd rather not think any more about tonight, thank you. If I had the power, I'd erase the whole day from my memory. But of course, we don't get to have any powers that would make *our* lives better.

I escape to my room when we get home, but the memories of the evening follow me in through the closed door, crowding around in a crushing mass. I shove away the images of Cadie, and of Cadie and Flynn, leaving only Flynn—handing me the bracelet, smiling at me on the Ferris wheel, joking in the fun house.

Holding my hand.

I'm still wearing the bracelet, but I yank it off and toss it into my mermaid wastebasket, future landfill fodder. I kick off my boots, crawl into bed and call Posh. I don't need to talk; I just want to lie here and listen to her ramble on about some new superconductor or nuclear fission chamber she's read about online, her nonsensical words knitting together until they settle over me like a warm blanket.

"Delaney!" Posh shrieks when she answers. "Guess who's over? Christopher Marlin!" The nerd from chess club? Fish face? With the potbelly and the buzz cut? Since when are he and Posh friends? "We were in the Princeton class together. I told you, didn't I? Mom said we can stay up in the backyard and watch the Eta Aquarids. They're tonight. Did you get my email? You've got to check them out."

She goes on about all the supplies they've gathered: lounge chairs, quilts, pretzels, root beer, and of course a sky chart and a stopwatch so they can time the intervals between the shooting stars and keep notes. "The Eta Aquarids aren't as good as the Perseids, but Christopher says too many meteors get boring after a while, because there's no thrill of anticipation."

I can't believe it. Posh has a boyfriend. Posh! "That's really great!" I don't sound like myself at all. I'm like a windup doll set on "chirpy."

Posh says something I can't hear and I know she's talking to Christopher. "Can I call you tomorrow?" she asks me.

"I've got something to do, but I'll call you next week." It won't matter if I don't, though. Posh has Christopher now. And he's *there*.

After I hang up, I gaze up at my constellation of earring stars. Tonight they seem as distant as real stars. At the far end of the galaxy. Completely out of reach. I will one to break free and shoot down to me, a meteor from Mom to tell me she's watching over me. But it doesn't come.

I hear my door open and I roll onto my side, curling into a ball. "Go away."

Dad comes in anyway. The bed dips as he sits down next to me. "I know something's wrong, Delaney." I don't answer. "Does it have to do with Flynn? Was he there tonight?"

"Nothing's wrong with Flynn. Everything's great. He got his wish."

Dad rests a hand on my shoulder. "It's hard sometimes, seeing other people happy when you're not. It's one of the biggest drawbacks to the job."

"You don't understand."

I shrug my shoulder so he'll lift his hand away. I wait for him to leave, but he stays. "Explain it to me, then."

"I wish Mom were here."

Dad's silent for a second, then he pats my arm. "I know. I'm sorry. I wish she were too." He stands. "Get some sleep. Things will look better in the morning." Why do people always say this? Sure, the sun can cover up some of the gloom, but it doesn't last.

"And then it'll be night, and things will look bad again."

I sense Dad's smile, but he has no argument for my logic. Instead of saying anything, he leans over to kiss my forehead, like I'm a little girl. I don't stop him, because I *want* to be a little girl again, the one Flynn saw, the one I used to be, even if it's only for a minute. I want to belong in a pink frilly room filled with dolls and still believe in fairy-tale endings.

Dad turns off the light as he leaves, so there's only the Tinker Bell night-light. It casts a purply glow against the wall. "Good night, sweetheart," he says, and closes the door without making a sound.

I cling tight to the feeling of being young and clueless, but as I fall asleep, I sense it slipping away, and I know it'll be gone long before I wake up.

chapter twelve

Dad and I are back in the car, but the mood is the opposite of last night's. I am up. I am on. I am over it.

A couple of hours earlier, I was in bed, gazing blankly at the whitish-yellow sunlight searing my bedroom carpet. I lay like that for about twenty minutes before I realized I was awake. My dreams had been a mash of wings and stars and me being stretched by some invisible force, my limbs snapping back like bungee cords before I plummeted to the ground, my bed rising up to meet me at the last second.

When I finally got loose of the dream, I practically leapt out of bed, as if there was an energy force propelling me. I left all the draggy emotional stuff from last night behind, dead and buried forever under my tangled sheets.

I'd been recharged.

I bounced into breakfast and loaded up on all the sugar-coated animal and planetary shapes I could find.

"Want to slow down there a little, Delaney?" Dad watched me as he whipped up his egg-white omelet. "There *will* be other meals in the day."

"I'm bulking up. So I'm ready for my next client."

"It probably won't be for a while. They're usually pretty spread out at the beginning."

"Whatever." I refilled my bowl.

Dad set his plate down across from me. "This is quite a change from last night."

"I had, like, an ultra-epiphany: f.g.'s are the same as firefighters or ER doctors. Or nannies. Helping other people is our only purpose. I've got the power now. I'll have another client any second, you'll see. In the meantime, I'm doing small wishes nonstop. My goal is two hundred a week. To start."

Dad sat down and studied me in concern while I devoured the last of my milk-sogged bears. "You seem a little . . . manic."

"I've just eaten like three cups' worth of sugar."

Dad took a bite of his omelet and chewed, for way longer than it should've taken to grind up something that was half air.

"You know, Delaney, sometimes we react to unsettling

227

feelings by repressing them beneath a hyper, overcompensating sense of—"

"I don't need any psycho–Dr. Hank–alyzing, thank you. I'm not one of your sad 'clients.' I'm superhuman and superfine."

"Nobody's superhuman, Delaney. We're all subject to bouts of depression, insecurity—"

I popped up from the table. "You're not listening to me. I'm beyond that. I have a wand." I held up my spoon, then took it to the sink along with the bowl. "Can we go to the mall early? I want to rack up some wishes before the signing. Get my numbers up."

"I have to go over to Andrea's first."

"You told her you'd talk to her Monday."

"I know, but she called this morning. She's a mess."

"She's always a mess. She's always going to *be* a mess."

"She needs help, Delaney. Didn't you just say a minute ago that helping people is our purpose? I'll pick you up after."

He was right. Andrea did need help. Extreme help. The help of a master.

"I'm coming with you."

★ ★ ★

So now here we are, pulling up in front of Andrea's apartment complex again. It's a repeat of our first f.g. outing, except this time it's during the day and there's none of the jasmine-scented eeriness of that night. The sunshine has stripped the magic and mystery away.

Andrea's calmed down a lot, but she still looks like a wreck, with her tangled hair, bleached-out, stretched-out cardigan and bunny slippers with cat-chewed ears.

"I texted Aaron this morning and told him that I passed out in the ladies' room and hit my head and got amnesia and ended up at an all-night clinic and didn't get my memory back until three a.m. and that's why I never came back to the table." Andrea barely breathes, her words tripping over each other as they come out of her mouth. "He offered to come over but I told him we should meet instead, so we're going to brunch! If you give me a spell *now*, it'll get me through the whole day and everything will be fine again."

Before Dad can say anything, I do.

"How is that going to work when you get married? You'll have to have Dad on speed dial." From Andrea's embarrassed expression, I can tell she already does. "That won't be enough, though. He'll have to move in with you." Andrea's eyes brighten for a second until she realizes I'm being sarcastic.

She turns to Dad, pleading. "I only need one day. I promise. I got out all the books. See?" She picks up a stack of Dad's books from the floor next to the couch. Sticky notes and bookmarks and scraps of paper poke out from the pages in every direction. "I'm going to read each one again, and—"

"That's not going to change anything," I tell her. Andrea looks to Dad for rescue.

"Delaney, that's enough," Dad says.

But it's not enough, and I'm not going to let him stop me before I've finished.

I walk over to Andrea and take hold of her arms so she has to face me. "Andrea. You're a stratospherically high-strung fashion disaster with no self-confidence." Andrea looks like she's about to burst into tears when I say this, while Dad seems on the verge of exploding into a lecture on manners, but I can't stop now. "Basically, you're a mess. But hey, that's who you are. Own it. Let Aaron see it."

Andrea cocks her head as my words seem to sink into her brain. Dad's expression has changed too as he absorbs what I've said. Even Andrea's cat tiptoes out from the kitchen to hear more. "Magic is just a superficial fix." I glance over at Dad when I say this. "Cinderella may have had the ball gown on when the prince fell in love with her, but he proposed to her when she was in rags."

"She didn't stay in rags, though," Andrea protests. "She became a princess and then she had the gowns again, lots more of them—"

"Okay, never mind, I take it back. This isn't a fairy tale. You don't need a ball gown and glass slippers to go to brunch. Just a sundress and some flip-flops." The cat slinks around Andrea's ankles, agreeing with me. I guide Andrea over to a tarnished mirror hanging on the wall. "Be yourself," I tell her. "Your whole self." Andrea's eyes meet mine in the mirror. "Let your hidden depths come out, whatever they are. If Aaron doesn't like the real you, it was never going to last longer than a spell anyway."

Andrea shifts her gaze to her own eyes. The near-tears expression is gone, replaced by a curious, thoughtful one. She seems to straighten up a little, and her stare grows hard, like a challenge.

"Drop us a text, let us know how it goes." I grab Dad's hand and pull him to the door.

"Shouldn't we—"

"Nope," I tell him. "She's got it now. It's up to her." As we leave, I catch Andrea's eyes in the mirror one more time, and she gives me a little smile. She's not there yet, but she's on her way.

★ ★ ★

We stop at a burrito shack on the way home, and I order two with everything plus an extra side of chips, because I am ravenous. It's as if that huge breakfast I ate never happened.

"That was great!" I announce between bites. "Andrea wasn't even my client and I got her the big wish. *Without* using my wand."

Dad picks the tortilla strips off his taco salad. "It's not over yet."

"It will be." I glance around for some small wishes to grant. I may not always need the magic, but it's like a first-aid kit—a good thing to have in emergencies, and it's best if it's fully stocked. "Feel free to thank me anytime."

Dad shakes his head, but not at me. "All these books I've written, telling people how to change themselves—when that's not the problem at all. I should give everyone their money back."

"It's *from* your book," I tell him. "*Be Your Own Life Coach*. Don't you remember?" Dad gazes above my head, like maybe the book will suddenly appear, floating in midair. "Chapter Five: 'Aim High, but Accept Your Basic Loserness.'"

Dad's gaze lowers to meet my eyes. "I don't think I've ever used the word 'loserness,' Delaney."

"Whatever. It was something like that. It goes on and on about how you have to work with your limitations or they'll turn against you, and how you can't win a battle with yourself. Blah, blah, snooze."

Dad shakes his head again, this time in amazement. "I can't believe you read my books."

"Somebody had to. Andrea's obviously forgotten what she read, and you don't remember what you wrote."

"You're right. I did forget. I've been trying to make my clients . . . different from how they are."

"Everybody's screwed up in some way, but they get even more screwed up if they try to change themselves." Forget transferring objects and manipulating atoms. *This* has been the biggest f.g. lesson I've learned so far.

Dad smiles. "How did you get to be so smart?"

I shrug. "Experience. You know what I did to get Flynn his wish? Nothing. I just . . . left him alone." My voice cracks a little on the last word, and the night comes flooding back like it happened two minutes ago, every pang of emotion fresh. I force the memory away and bite down on another chip, but it must be stale, because it's like cardboard in my mouth. I load the next one with salsa, but the salsa's lost its taste too.

I notice Dad watching me with the same concerned look he had this morning. "That's what this is all about, isn't it? I thought so."

"What are you talking about?"

"Does Flynn know how you feel?"

I can't speak for a second. When I do, I pretend that I have no idea what he means. "Feel about what?"

"Feel about *him*."

"I need some new salsa." I start to stand, but Dad takes my hand and pulls me back to my seat.

"Delaney. Talk to me."

"I think you're confused," I say calmly. "I have no emotional attachment to Flynn. Our relationship was strictly professional. He's in love with Cadie, remember? If you don't believe me, you can go to her boffo beach blast and look for them, making out in the surf." I yank loose from his grasp and gather up my food. My appetite is officially gone.

"Were you invited to the party?"

Really, this conversation should be over by now. "I'm not going to any stupid beach party. Did you forget about your book signing?"

Dad keeps talking like he doesn't hear me. "You know

what? It doesn't matter if you were invited or not." He follows me as I carry my food to the trash. "You have to go, Delaney. And you have to tell him."

"Why? So I can be humiliated? I'm not his wish." I weave through the tables to the parking lot, concentrating on the mental wall I'm holding up to keep my feelings penned in, where they can't do any more damage.

"If he knew how you felt, he might change his mind."

We get into the car and I slam the door. "No, he wouldn't. She's *Cadie*."

"And you're Delaney." He smiles at me. A kind, fatherly smile, and it reminds me of Mom, and how she'd look at me sometimes as if she were viewing me through those soft-focus glasses that make parents think their child is the smartest or the prettiest or whatever-est. It's nice, even if it's wrong, and I don't like that it starts to make me sad all over again.

"Don't use me as a role model, Delaney," Dad says. "Don't use being a fairy godmother as an excuse to cut yourself off from other people. It may be too late for me, but it's not too late for you."

I don't respond. Suddenly I don't have the strength to speak or even move. All the hyped-up energy I had at the beginning of the day has drained away. As we drive out of the lot, I just want to get home and sleep for a hundred years.

★ ★ ★

I can't sleep, though, because I have to go to the signing. When we got home from the taco stand, I told Dad

234

that it was important to me to go, because this was a part of his life I'd never gotten to share before now. This was the perfect thing to say, because he instantly forgot all about Flynn and the beach party and started to tell me a bunch of stories about his signings from the past, all of which sounded beyond dull. I'm sure this one will be just as deadly, but at least it'll be a distraction.

Before we leave, I tell Dad I have a present for him. (I've decided to embrace the local custom of gifts-for-no-reason.) I meet him in the living room and hand him a small box. Dad opens it and takes out a pair of star-shaped cuff links I found at one of the yard sales. There weren't any with magic wands on them, but I figured this was close.

"Wow, I haven't worn cuff links since . . . I'm not sure I've ever worn them."

"It's never too late to try something new."

He smiles. "Thank you, honey." He gives me a kiss on the cheek. "I have something for you too." He hands me a shopping bag from Vogel's, the department store at the mall. "I hope I did better on this than I did on the bed-room."

Oh God, what if it's some plaid jumper, or a khaki skirt with a pink sweater twinset? Or a cute sundress with little bow ties on the shoulders? Dad's smile is so eager and anxious that I vow not to retch no matter how hideously un-me it is. It'll be easy enough to spill something on it "accidentally" so I don't have to wear it.

I lift out the gold-tissue-wrapped item, and the sparkly

paper crinkles as I unfold it. It's a dress. Not a sundress or a jumper, though, and it's not pink or any other pastel color—but it's not black either. Instead it's dark green, the color of a forest at night, with slashes of fiery red and yellow like comet tails all over it. I hold it up and it hits mid-thigh, perfect for boots. The material is slinky and soft.

"Well? What do you think?" When I drop the dress back in the bag, Dad looks worried, until I run over to him and hug him.

"I love it." I do. It's nothing I'd ever think to buy or even try on, and yet, somehow, he knew it was exactly right for me. Dad's arms wrap around me, strong and tight in a real hug, our first, the one I've been waiting for since before I can remember, and it's like a spell I didn't even know I was under breaks. I'm stepping free from something dark, with teeth, that's been holding on to me.

Weirdly, it feels like Mom is hugging me too, and it's really great. Sad, but not the usual "I want to set off a nuclear bomb and wipe out everybody" sad. Instead it's "this is a part of me now and I'm almost okay with it" sad. The kind of sad that can still let some happy in.

★ ★ ★

By the time we get to the bookstore, I'm glad I've come. It'll keep my mind off other things. I may have been crazy this morning, but I wasn't wrong. I need to stay focused on *other people*. Today it's Dad.

When we get upstairs to the events area, there's already a crowd. The chairs are all taken and more people squeeze in at the back. I grab a seat at the café, where I can watch the action from afar.

I prop my boots up on a chair and admire the way the dress drapes over my knees. They're the boots I wore on the plane. The yellow swirls match the yellow slashes on the dress, and for once I'm not horrified at being color-coordinated, because it feels like the boots and dress were made for each other. It's not a ball gown and glass slippers, but there *is* something a little magical about it, like part of my past with Mom has mixed with my future with Dad.

Dad's fans swarm him as soon as they see him, until Gina and the assistant manager shoo them away and back to their seats. Gina and Dad say hello but they barely look at each other. Not good.

After Dad reads a passage from the book, he throws in some new advice, "inspired by an important lesson I relearned today." He smiles my way. "A lesson I'd forgotten in my quest to change everyone on the planet for the better." The crowd laughs on cue. He recites a version of what I said to Andrea, but he's translated it into life coach—ese, and he wraps it up with: "Remember, only *you* can be you, and you can only be *you*." Leave it to Dad to make something simple ultraconvoluted, but his fans obviously speak "Dr. Hank," because they all clap and ooh and make a mental note to reserve a copy of the next book as soon as the publication date is announced.

After the reading, everybody presses in to buy the new book and get their millisecond one-on-one consult with Dr.

Hank, along with his priceless autograph. As Gina hands Dad each book, she watches him with the faraway wistful expression I saw on Cadie's face, and I know Gina still likes him. He lectured me on the way over about not trying to push them together again, but he warned me too late. I'd already made the call.

From the café, I have a clear view of the escalator, which I've had one eye on since we got here, and now I see them rise up like angels into the cookbooks and crafts section. They step off, holding hands. She's wearing a soda-pop-orange sundress and aqua flip-flops. He's skinny, with long, rock star hair. He's not what I imagined at all, but they look exactly right for each other.

I'd snagged Dad's cell from his jacket pocket at the end of our big hug. It was an impulse, something I knew I needed to do. When I went back to my room to put on the dress, I found Andrea's number in the address book and dialed.

"Dr. Hank! I love you!" she squealed when she answered, so loud I had to quickly shut my door so Dad wouldn't hear. After I told Andrea it was me, she launched into another Posh-worthy breathless speed-of-light report about how Aaron had listened to her confession of her hang-ups and then confessed that he'd been afraid to show *his* true self with her, even after he proposed, because he was so intimidated whenever she'd show up for their dates in her fancy f.g.-spell-generated designer dresses and chic hairstyles.

Andrea spots me and starts for the café, but I shake

my head and point to Dad, who's giving brow-furrowed advice to one of his devotees. Andrea and Aaron get in line, and I spoon up the remaining sugary-spicy foam from the bottom of my cup and wait. Gina notices Andrea first and gets an alarmed look on her face. She glances around, searching, like the store's got a lunatic wrangler on staff for these sorts of situations. Too late, though, because Andrea's already stepped up to Dad, who now wears the same tense expression as Gina. Andrea talks, bouncing up and down in her flip-flops, waving one hand in the air while the other clutches Aaron's. Dad's face slowly transforms from anxious to relieved to delighted. As Andrea showers her words over Dad and Gina, Gina's worry softens into a smile.

It's like a silent movie, since I'm too far away to hear. The best part of the story comes when Gina and Dad both laugh at the same time, and their eyes meet, and their gaze hangs on for a few seconds like they've been caught in some invisible force field. Once again, no magic required— except for the kind that comes naturally.

The movie continues to play and my eyes zoom in, like a camera, on Andrea and Aaron, and then on their hands, still clasped. My right hand is suddenly warm, as if someone has taken hold of it, but when I look down, it's empty. I still feel it, though, or remember the feeling, or feel the memory, or whatever.

Time seems to speed up, and then slow down, and then it reverses, as the day up to now runs through my mind. Then the last few days, and then the last few weeks, and then the months. Then I'm back here in the bookstore, and I start to think. . . .

No. I can't think. I'm done with thinking. It gives me a headache.

I concentrate on the Brennan's logo on my latte cup, not allowing thoughts to stick, willing them to float away and disappear, exactly like Ms. Byrd teaches us to do in yoga.

But one thought turns around midflight, and before I can stop it, it comes zinging back and lands, *bang*. It latches on to me, and it's not going to let go.

I have to do it. I have to try.

I must blank out then, because I'm not aware of getting up or walking over to Dad or interrupting the lovefest going on around Andrea and Aaron, which the customers have now joined in on. I am just already *there*, and I tell Dad something that people here in the land of omnipresent sunshine say all the time.

"I want to go to the beach."

★ ★ ★

We drive along the coast, windows down. The glowing terra-cotta sun lounges in the late-afternoon sky, its big butt dropping so near the darkening blue-green of the ocean it's like it wants to plop in already and cool off. There's no end to the earth, and anything seems possible.

We couldn't leave until the signing was finished, and although Dad tried to wrap things up fast, there was always somebody with one last question, and it felt like it took hours to get out of there. Cadie's party could already be over, which, as we get closer, I start to wish for, because it will be like getting the "no" without having to be emotionally stomped on in public.

But when Dad pulls up to the steps that lead down to the beach, I can see Mia and some of the other kids from school playing volleyball. As I get out of the car, I hear hip-hop from someone's radio, and I spot more kids scattered around, on towels or in the water.

"Do you want me to wait?" This is the first thing Dad's said the whole trip. There was nothing to say before, really. He knows why I've come.

"That's okay. I've got my cell." I tap the pocket at the top of one of my boots. "Or I'll come find you. You're only going to be over there."

I point toward the pier farther down the beach, where crowded outdoor tables at a Mexican restaurant overlook boardwalkers, arcade players, merry-go-round riders, ice cream eaters and the sea. Dad's having dinner at the restaurant with Gina after she gets off work. It was her idea. She suggested it after I made my announcement, unaware that my reasons for wanting to go to the beach weren't recreational.

I insisted that they go anyway, without me, and after making sure I was sure, Dad agreed. Andrea and Aaron were included in the invitation, so it's not really a date. It's a start, though, a fresh one. With Andrea there, it'd be a great opportunity to get the whole f.g. secret identity thing out on the table, but I'm not going to mention this to Dad. His life's up to him now.

Like mine is up to me.

As Dad drives off, I scope out the crowd, but the big fireball sun has turned most of the beach partyers into silhouettes.

When I reach the bottom of the wooden stairs, I realize that the sand will ruin my boots—I'm going to have to carry them. I grab the railing and unzip one, then the other. I feel naked without them, like a turtle without its shell, a knight without his armor, any other fill-in-the-blank metaphor for agonizing vulnerability you want to come up with.

The hot sand grabs hold of my feet with every step, and I'm already regretting this. He's not here anyway. I don't see him. I might as well leave.

But then—there he is, sitting on a towel a few yards up from the surf, legs straight out, leaning back on his hands. He's staring ahead to where I can barely make out two figures doing what can only be called frolicking in the cascading waves at the edge of the shore, laughing and splashing each other with foamy salt water.

One is tan and lean and wearing a neon yellow bikini, her long wet hair plastered over her shoulders like mermaid's locks. Guess who?

What was I thinking? Oh, that's right—I wasn't thinking. Why not? Why *didn't* I think? Now I'm going to have to get out of here before anyone sees me, and that means going back through the quicksand, which is anything but quick.

"Delaney?"

Flynn is squinting up at me over his shoulder. How did he know I was here? And how did he manage to peel his eyes away from his beloved sea nymph?

He scrambles up from the towel and trots over to me, and somehow his feet don't sink like mine. There must be a trick to walking on California sand.

He's got on long board shorts and smells like sunscreen and sweat. I notice that he's in pretty good shape for a yearbook geek. He's no Mr. Muscle or anything, but he doesn't need to cover up.

"I didn't think you were coming. Where's your bathing suit?"

"I was just passing by."

Flynn studies me. "You look different."

"No boots," I say, and hold them up. I feel embarrassed by my bare legs, even though they're the least bare of anyone's here. My face gets red, but at least the sun is casting a pink glow over everything so no one will notice. Especially Flynn.

"I bet they look great with that dress," he says. "But the dress looks nice without them too," he adds quickly. "It's a nice dress."

Flynn grins in a goofy, awkward way. The heat from my cheeks flushes through to my sand-clamped toes. I didn't even know a full-body blush was possible. Really, what is the point of this torture? Doesn't he realize that having two boots in my hands means that I'm armed?

Instead of using my boots as weapons, I pull myself together. This is the new Delaney Collins, who puts her professional responsibilities first. When I look at Flynn right now, through f.g. eyes, I do truly want him to have his wish.

"I just came by to say congratulations," I tell him. "I really am happy for you."

Flynn puts his hands on his hips and cocks his head at me. "What are you talking about? Congratulations for what?"

"You and Cadie." I gesture out beyond the surf, where Cadie is now one of several bobbing heads waiting for a wave.

Flynn gives me a strange look. "You mean you don't know?" Know what? "Cadie said you were the one who told her to be herself," he says.

"Yeah, so?"

Behind Flynn, Cadie bodysurfs to shore, followed by her fellow frolicker—the tag-along girl from last night, Emma. They push themselves up and slap the sand off each other's legs, laughing. Their hands meet and they stop.

They straighten up, hands still touching. Their fingers intertwine and they stare at each other as the water ebbs and flows around their ankles. I notice that Emma's bathing suit is covered in drawings of dragonflies.

Finally I get it—but I don't get it, because how could I not know this? I'm supposed to have extrasensory f.g. perception.

"So that's *not* her cousin," I say, to myself as much as to Flynn. Observation + calculation = conclusion.

"No."

The volleyballers have run down to the water, and I watch Mia pause as she nears Cadie and Emma, who quickly let go of each other's hands. All three stand uneasily. Mia says something and then Cadie does. Mia touches Cadie's arm and they both seem to relax a little; then Mia darts off and dives into the water.

Cadie puts her arm around Emma's shoulder, and they walk away, along the jagged rim of the ocean, where wet sand meets dry, into the sunset, a Hollywood ending.

"Wow" is all I can say.

"Yeah."

I feel Flynn watching me. I'm thrown off balance for a second and I have to take a step to the side, bracing myself. It's back. That churning, yearning, queasy, woozy sensation. Am I getting another client already? What happened to my promised break? There's no one around, though, except Flynn.

"You still like her." This is beyond pathetically tragic, for too many reasons.

So why is Flynn laughing?

"Are you kidding? I never liked Cadie. If it wasn't for your short-circuited voodoo magic-radar 'you belong together' nagging, I wouldn't have even thought it. I told you way back at the start, you got it all wrong."

"Then who?" I glance up and down the beach. God, I hope it's not Mia. She may not be completely evil, but she'd still squash him like a bug.

Flynn laughs again, a lighter laugh this time that blends with the whoosh of the waves. Like at the book signing, the memory of Flynn holding my hand returns, but sand and sweat press against my palm too, and when I look down, his hand really is there, in mine.

It takes centuries for my eyes to lift, all the way up, to meet his. He's still smiling, a crooked, nervous, adorable smile. We don't say anything, we just stand and stare.

The sounds around us separate: the crashing of the waves, the caws of gulls, the voices of swimmers, the wind. Then they blend again, and the seasick feeling pulls away, gone at last, like the tide going out, leaving only a tired, happy sort of calm.

Is this what it feels like when you grant someone's wish? Or when you get your own?

★　★　★

There's a Ferris wheel on the pier. We rise up, and although I can't see Dad or Gina or Andrea or Aaron, I know they're down there, somewhere, with all the rest of the people in the world. Flynn holds my boots on the other side of him, so we can sit close, and his leg presses against mine, our bare skin touching.

At the top, we stop. Flynn looks over at me with his

"X-raying the soul" photographer expression. Except it's softened by a smile, just for me. Before he gets any closer, before any other parts of our bodies touch, I have to get it over with. I'm not going to make Dad's mistake. I'm not going to hide. I'm going to be honest from the start.

"There's something I have to tell you. About me." He probably won't believe me, but I'll be able to prove it to him soon enough, once my next client comes along.

"Okay." He focuses on me, serious, listening.

"It's a long story."

Flynn peers down, making the car swing, then smiles up at me. "I'm not going anywhere."

Suddenly I'm nervous. I'm not sure what to say next. I don't know where to begin.

The last purple crescent of sun falls into the sea, off duty at last, and I glance up, where stars will soon appear, like they always do. I search the sky for an answer. The twilight is so magical and unreal that I think I spot a glimmer of a star already. When I turn back to Flynn, it's like the star has stayed in my view, because I see a glow on the other side of him—but it's not a star. It's coming from one of my boots. Or rather, from the chopstick sticking out of the holster.

A chopstick that's become a wand.

Then it hits me all at once and I laugh to myself. I know exactly what to say next, because, really, there's only one way *to* begin.

"Once upon a time . . ."

If **KATHY MCCULLOUGH** had one wish, it would be for world peace—or a continuously replenishing bar of chocolate. A graduate of Cornell University, she lives in Los Angeles, where she works as a novelist and screenwriter. This is her first book. Visit Kathy online at kathymcculloughbooks.com or follow her on Twitter @kathymccullough.